KICK START

orca sports

KICK START

MICHELE MARTIN BOSSLEY

ORCA BOOK PUBLISHERS

Library and Archives Canada Cataloguing in Publication

Title: Kick start / Michele Martin Bossley.
Names: Bossley, Michele Martin, author.
Series: Orca sports.

Description: Series statement: Orca sports

Identifiers: Canadiana (PRINT) 20190070854 |
Canadiana (EBOOK) 20190070862 | ISBN 9781459818132 (SOFTCOVER) |
ISBN 9781459818149 (PDF) | ISBN 9781459818156 (EPUB)

Classification: LCC PS8553.O7394 K53 2019 | DDC jC813/.54—dc23

Library of Congress Control Number: 2019934031
Simultaneously published in Canada and the United States in 2019

Summary: In this high-interest novel for young readers, Mitch has to
win an upcoming race in order to keep his new dirt bike.

*Orca Book Publishers is committed to reducing the consumption
of nonrenewable resources in the making of our books. We make
every effort to use materials that support a sustainable future.*

Orca Book Publishers gratefully acknowledges the support for its
publishing programs provided by the following agencies: the Government of
Canada, the Canada Council for the Arts and the Province of British Columbia
through the BC Arts Council and the Book Publishing Tax Credit.

Edited by Tanya Trafford
Cover photograph by istock.com/vm
Author photo by Randy Allcock, Village Studio

ORCA BOOK PUBLISHERS
orcabook.com

Printed and bound in Canada.

22 21 20 19 • 4 3 2 1

*To Shelby Turner,
the rider who inspired this story.*

*And to the memory of
Calahan Bruder. Your racing friends
will never forget you.*

Chapter One

"This is going to be great!" Uncle Jamie rubbed his hands together. The low thrum of engines and sudden revving of throttles was like music across the gravel parking lot.

I shut the car door and looked around. Campers and utility trailers jammed the edges of the parking lot, dust and grit blew in the air, and the smell of oil and gas floated on the breeze.

"Yeah," I agreed. "It is!" We started toward Calgary's racetrack. I stared at the dirt bikes in front of the trailers as we passed.

Every make and model I'd ever heard of seemed to be here. This was motorcycle heaven.

"Your dad and I rode those when we first started racing enduro." Uncle Jamie pointed to a red-and-white dirt bike. "We had 150s. They were gutsy little bikes. Could go up anything."

"I know. Dad told me."

"Mitch, you still have the 65 we fixed up for you? Man, your dad and I put in some hours trying to get that running for you."

"Yeah. It's in the corner of the shed. I'm way too big for it now."

Uncle Jamie looked at my lanky frame. "I'd say so. You rode that when you were nine years old. What are you now, eleven?"

"Thirteen." I grinned. "Ha. Like you weren't at my birthday two weeks ago."

"Yeah, but I have a bad memory." Uncle Jamie slung an arm across my shoulders. "Or maybe I just don't want to you to grow up. Means I'm getting old."

"Hey, Jamie!" a voice called out. "Is that you, old man?" A short guy with a huge smile came out from behind a trailer. He stepped around the bike parts that littered the grass and wiped his black-stained hands on a greasy rag.

"Darren! I thought you might be here!" The two gave each other a back-slapping hug. "It's been too long, man."

"Well, you quit racing, dude. You have to get back on the circuit!" Darren said, grinning at my uncle.

"Maybe sometime," Uncle Jamie said. "Work is busy, and I don't have a bike."

"I can set you up. Come by the shop sometime. Still in the same place. Lethbridge isn't that far."

"Sounds good to me. You racing this weekend?"

"Yeah, in the old guys' class tomorrow. I wanted to watch the pros today, and I brought Kelsey up. Her mom and dad are seeding on the farm, so it was too much time away for them to come."

"Kelsey?" I said.

"Kelsey Murray. She's the best female rider in Canada right now, and she's only fifteen.

She's racing Intermediate Men's today. There isn't anyone in the women's classes who can even touch her."

"Wow." Uncle Jamie looked impressed.

"She's racing in about fifteen minutes, so if you want to see her, better get down to the track," Darren said, pointing past his trailer to the crowd of people moving down the gravel road. "Look for number 19."

"Okay, see you later!" Uncle Jamie steered me behind a group of kids who looked younger than me and had clearly raced earlier in the day. They wore heavy boots and brightly colored fabric dirt-biking pants with leather patches on the inside of the legs at the knee. Their thin jerseys were generally the same colors as the pants, but not always. One girl wore purple-and-bright-green pants with a yellow jersey. I could tell this group had already raced because their faces and jerseys were streaked with dust and sweat. Their boots and pants were caked with hardened mud. They were joking with each other and laughing. I kind of wished I could hang

4

out with them. It looked like they were having fun.

Uncle Jamie headed toward the starting line. Racers were already gathering. The track looked difficult. I didn't know how the riders were supposed to get over the massive logs and through the rock sections, let alone navigate some of the huge jumps. The water section looked the easiest. It was already churned into a mud bath. Endurocross is different than motocross, because enduro has a lot of obstacles you have to ride through, plus jumps. Motocross has shorter courses with mostly different kinds of jumps.

The announcer started talking over the loudspeaker, but we were so close, I couldn't make out what he was saying. The riders on the line pumped the kick-starters with their right feet. They twisted the throttles. Each rider seemed to be trying to outdo the others, revving their engines. The noise was incredible. A man in front gestured with his arms to get them to cut their engines.

An immediate silence fell.

"All right. You guys know the rules. It's a dead start—hands on your helmet," the man shouted. "When I wave the flag, you start your engine and go. Okay?" The man stepped to the side and waited until everyone had positioned themselves. The riders put their goggles on and placed their gloved hands on the top of their helmets. I saw number 19. If it weren't for the light-brown braid that swung down beneath her helmet, I wouldn't even have known she was a girl. Her bike wasn't as flashy as some of the others, and she wore gear that was mostly black and gray with some red. She didn't exactly stand out in that crowd of crazy colors.

The man lifted the flag above his head. I held my breath. The flag flapped downward, and the engines exploded to life. I barely even saw the riders kick-start their bikes again, they were that fast. Number 19 darted off the line, just ahead of two other riders. She kicked the bike up a notch and disappeared around the first bend in a cloud of dust.

"Kelsey got the holeshot!" Uncle Jamie nudged me with his elbow. "That's awesome!"

"What?" I said.

"The holeshot. The first rider off the line that holds the lead. It doesn't necessarily mean you'll win, but it's bragging rights after the race," Uncle Jamie explained.

"Oh." I coughed in the dusty air, which now swirled around the crowd. All the riders were gone, except for one poor dude who was kicking and kicking at his starter. Finally the bike roared out of its coma and the rider took off, trying to catch up to the others.

"Let's go over to the other side of the track," Uncle Jamie said. "We can watch them go through the logs and the rocks. The big tabletop is over there."

I knew the tabletop was a type of jump that inclined hard on one side and had a long flat section in the middle before it sloped downward again. It was supposed to be tricky, because the rider had to catch a lot of air in the middle of the jump to make the decline on the other side. You absolutely did not want to come down hard from a jump on a flat surface. That was just asking for a crash.

We walked through the dirt, on pathways that had been worn in by people making their way to the rocks and logs sections. The first riders were already going through. I saw number 19 navigating the rocks. She made it look easy. Her bike climbed slowly over each rock, her back tire dropping down into the crevices, but her balance didn't waver once. As she hit the last rock, she sped up, heading for the tabletop. Her bike soared into the air. It honestly looked like she was flying. She had to have been at least twenty feet in the air. The bike sailed over the tabletop and landed smoothly, rolling down the decline and into the dip. Kelsey gassed it, and the bike flew up the next jump, into the air and down. There was a rhythm to it, like music.

"She's really got the flow," Uncle Jamie said. "That kid's got some real talent."

I just nodded, awed by what I was seeing. Rider after rider took the jumps, trying to catch Kelsey.

One guy on an orange bike rode aggressively through the rocks, then up on the logs like it was no problem at all. I recognized him as the guy who had had trouble getting his bike going at the starting line. He'd made up a lot of time. He was only about five places behind Kelsey, with still a lot of time left in the race. He had to be pretty good.

I watched him finish the log section and accelerate through the corner, toward the tabletop. He hit the throttle and rocketed upward, but I could tell right away that something was wrong. He was going way too fast. His body twisted above the seat, and the bike's front end edged sideways. It should have been heading straight. The dirt bike overshot the jump, and my eyes widened in horror as I saw the rider separate from the bike. In midair, the rider shoved the bike away from himself.

The bike smashed down well past the landing area. Small parts flew like confetti.

The bike tumbled end-over-end and dropped like a dead thing on its side. The handlebars and frame were bent. If the fierce buzzing of the other bikes hadn't been so loud, I was sure I would have heard the screeching tear of metal.

The rider hit the edge of the jump feet-first. He tucked in his shoulder and rolled down the slope, eventually coming to rest in the dirt at the bottom.

He lay facedown, very still.

Chapter Two

A horrified gasp rose from the crowd. The rider wasn't moving, but if he didn't get off the track soon, he was in danger of being run over.

Two race officials bolted over the barricades. A third was frantically waving a flag farther up the track to warn the other racers that a rider was down. As the two officials bent to help him, the rider twitched and lifted his head. He shook it, then slowly raised himself up on his elbows, then his knees. The officials clearly were talking to him, and within seconds they had him up on his feet. They helped him get off the track.

The crowd began to clap and cheer. A few men pulled the twisted wreck of the dirt bike off the track and rolled it along the edge of the crowd.

The race continued, but I watched the injured rider. His helmet and chest protector were removed. Paramedics checked him over, but he waved them off. He sat still for a while, drinking a bottle of water, talking to people who came over. But he kept glancing over toward his dirt bike. Even from where I was, I could tell he was really mad.

My uncle tapped my shoulder. "Kelsey's in first!" he shouted in my ear over the buzzing of the motors.

I saw her colors flash by as she took the jump in front us. Then the rest of the riders whizzed past, one after another in a blur. The jumps became a dance, and the rhythm flowed through every rider. But the rocks and logs stopped everyone, like stubbing a toe. When the riders got through, the dance started again.

The final lap rushed past. On the final turn, a rider passed Kelsey. She sailed through the last jump and the checkered flag in second place.

"What an awesome race!" Uncle Jamie yelled. "Way to go, Kelsey!" he bellowed across the track.

"She did pretty good for a girl," I said.

Uncle Jamie turned to me. "She did pretty good for anybody," he said. "Not because she's a girl. That girl could kick your butt so hard you wouldn't know where to find it."

"Well, obviously," I said. "I haven't ridden a dirt bike in almost three years. Of course she's better than me." I shook my head. "I didn't mean, you know, that I expected her to do worse because she's a girl."

"Yeah, you did. But Kelsey's riding with all the guys, and she's better than most of them. So just remember that when you meet her."

"We're going to meet her?" I felt a moment of panic. I never know what to say to girls, let alone one who could kick my butt.

"Yeah. Let's go find Darren before they start the next heat." Uncle Jamie began to push through the sidelines.

I hung back. As the crowd thinned to take a break before the next race, I saw the rider who had crashed walk toward his wrecked dirt bike. He was with another rider, one who clearly hadn't raced yet. His outfit was still clean.

"This bike is destroyed," said his friend. "I'm not sure it's worth the money to fix it."

The rider kicked his bike tire angrily. "I wish I could get someone to buy it. I need a decent bike. I've tweaked this one and replaced just about every stupid part. I still can't win on it."

"No one would buy this piece of junk," said his friend. "It's completely trashed."

"I'd buy it," I said. I had no idea why I'd spoken. Had I completely lost my mind?

They both glanced up. "Who are you?"

"Mitch Harding."

"Why would you want this? It's scrap metal, dude," said the friend.

"I used to ride a lot with my dad, and my bike is too small. I haven't got much money to buy a new one, that's for sure."

"If you've got two thousand bucks, it's yours," said the rider.

"Deal." I stuck out my hand, and we shook on it. My mom had made me save almost everything I had made from my paper route since I was nine. I knew I had close to two thousand dollars in my savings account. She was going to flip out when she found out I'd blown it all, but I knew this was the only way I could get a bike. And it was a good bike. This rider was racing on it, right? He was practically a pro—it had to be good.

So it would need a few repairs. How hard could that be?

Chapter Three

"You did *what*?" Uncle Jamie said.

"I bought that guy's bike. The racer who crashed."

"Mitch, that's a huge purchase, man. You don't just buy a bike, especially one that you can't even ride. How do you know you can even get it running?"

"Well, I thought you might help me with that."

"You did, did you?" Uncle Jamie gave me a small smile. "I guess I wouldn't mind, but your mom is going to fry my butt for letting you do this. I think we should go talk to this guy."

"But we already shook on it. I need to go get the money."

"Just hang on a minute. I want to have a look at the bike first," said Uncle Jamie firmly.

"I'll come too," Darren said. I'd found Uncle Jamie back at Darren's trailer, where they were fiddling with a new tube for a tire on a stand. He put down the tools he held and wiped his hands on an old rag before the three of us started back toward the track and the scene of the crash.

The rider and his friend were slugging back cold drinks. The cans dripped with condensation, making me wish I had one too. The heat had gotten more intense, giving everything a dry, dusty feel. "Hey," the rider greeted us. "You back from the bank already?"

"Not yet, Logan," Darren said. "Mitch is a little young to soak that kind of money into a bike without getting some advice first."

"Hey, I bought my first bike at four-teen," Logan answered. "We shook on it. A deal's a deal."

"Maybe so, but if it's not a fair deal, then we need to talk," Uncle Jamie said. "Let's have a look at this bike."

The race was over, and people had drifted away. It wasn't difficult to tug the bike away from the edge of the track and find a space to pull it upright.

"Well, the handlebars are twisted and the throttle is busted. Those will have to be replaced," Uncle Jamie said. "And the radiator is completely dented. The plastic is wrecked...I don't know."

Darren looked the bike over. "I think this thing is going to cost a bundle to fix. Mitch, are you sure you want to take on a job like this?"

"I can't afford a bike any other way," I said. "New bikes cost way too much."

"Yeah, but by the time you buy all the replacement parts and put in the time to fix it up, you'll probably end up spending more than you would have on a new bike."

Darren paused to glare at Logan. "Which is exactly why Logan is selling it to you."

Uncle Jamie rubbed his chin. "Maybe not."

"Huh?" Darren said.

"Maybe it won't cost as much as a new bike to fix if you and I help him. But it's going to mean customizing stuff and pulling parts off old bikes. Not exactly easy. And if we don't get it together and get it working, he'll only have a pile of scrap metal to sell. But Mitch did make a deal. And he shook on it. We're kind of stuck." Uncle Jamie turned to Logan. "How would you feel about adding a little extra to your deal? A little bet might even things up a bit."

"What kind of bet?" Logan said.

"If you tried to sell this pile of junk right now, you might get a thousand bucks for parts. Maybe. The plastic is cracked, your pipe is dented, the radiator needs to be replaced. The list is huge. Not all of this just happened when you crashed either. You've been racing this bike hard since the spring. So no one except a kid like Mitch is likely to see it being worth much. Mitch will pay you the two thousand dollars as agreed. But if he gets this bike up and running and can finish a race on it before the end of the season, you give him back half of his money. A thousand bucks."

Logan frowned. "Why would I do that?"

"Because it's fair," Darren said. "Because it's the right thing to do. You know you should have sold it to him for a thousand in the first place. You want your sponsors to know you swindled a kid?"

"Hey, he offered to buy it!" Logan protested.

"Yes, but you took advantage. This wager would give him an opportunity to get the bike at a fair price, *if* he can get it running," said Uncle Jamie. "And realistically, how likely is it that we can actually rebuild this bike?"

Logan eyed his bike. It was dripping fluid, barely upright even with Darren holding the bars. Anyone could see it was mortally wounded. "Okay, I'll take that bet," he said, holding out his hand. He and I shook on it.

"Thanks," I said.

"Good luck," Logan said with a sneer.

"We'll be back with your money shortly," Uncle Jamie said.

"How bad is it?" I whispered as he and I walked away.

"Pretty bad," Uncle Jamie said. "But I think Darren might give us a hand. He's got lots of parts he's pulled off old bikes in case he needed them. Maybe he'll let us have them for cheap."

"But I don't have any money left."

"I can help a bit. And when we tell your dad, maybe we can get him to fork over some cash."

"Mom is not going to like this," I said.

Uncle Jamie grinned. "Nope. But you should have thought of that before you agreed to buy a dirt bike without permission. Weren't you supposed to be saving that money for a laptop?"

Oooh. I'd forgotten about that. "Kind of, yeah."

"And here you go, putting fun before your education. Mitch, what are we going to do with you?" Uncle Jamie said, doing a very good impression of my mother.

I laughed. "Fix up a dirt bike so we can go riding?"

"Here's hoping." We reached the truck and Uncle Jamie unlocked it. "Hop in. Let's go get your money and get this bike home."

Chapter Four

The garage was littered with stuff. An old scooter, my bicycle, tools, Dad's dirt bike, my old 65 cc, a shop vac, the usual kind of things. I began shoving things in corners so we could unload my new dirt bike. Even though it was in pretty rough shape, I couldn't help feeling excited. It had been a long time since I'd been able to ride.

I found the steel ramp Dad always used to load and unload bikes from the truck. Uncle Jamie backed the truck up to the garage door and jumped out. He began to undo the straps, then climbed into the truck bed.

"Mitch, loosen the rest off while I hold it," he called down to me.

I pushed at the metal fastenings until the straps fell away from the bike. Uncle Jamie backed it down the ramp slowly. I grabbed it as it came down and steered it backward into the garage. Uncle Jamie hoisted it onto a bike stand, and we stood back to survey my new purchase. It didn't exactly look like my dream bike, that's for sure.

"Your mother is going to kill me," Uncle Jamie said.

"Well, she...uh...doesn't exactly know yet," I said.

"*What?*" Uncle Jamie raised his hands in the air. "I thought you called her from the track! Why didn't you tell her?" He moaned. "Now I'm really going to be in trouble!"

The inside door to the garage opened, and my mother appeared with a fistful of rags and a hammer in her hands. She looked at us suspiciously. "Who's in trouble?" she said. "And where did that heap of junk come from?" She waved at the dirt bike on the stand.

"Oh, nobody," I said. "And this...it's just something I brought home from the race."

"Something you brought home from the race," she said slowly. "What, like a souvenir?"

"Sort of." I grinned at her.

She shook her head. "It looks like a dirt bike to me. Tell me the whole story."

"One of the racers crashed it and wanted to sell it cheap, so I bought it."

"*How* cheap?" my mother asked.

"Two thousand dollars," I said.

"*That's not cheap!*" she cried. "Mitch! Where did you get the money?"

"From my savings, the paper route."

"Mitchell, that money was supposed to be for a laptop! Not a bunch of junk!" My mom glared at me. Then she turned to my uncle. "Jamie, how could you let him do that?"

"He had already made a deal with the guy when I got involved. They shook on it. What was I supposed to do?"

"Act like a parent and tell him that under no circumstances was this going to happen!" My mom was barely keeping her voice under control.

"Megan, I'm his uncle, not his dad. But if Matt were here, he'd probably have done the same thing," Uncle Jamie said quietly.

That stopped my mother.

"Look, the kid has to learn sometime. The bike needs major work. We know that. But I have some friends who are willing to donate parts or sell them to us cheap. Mitch can learn what it takes to fix a bike, take care of it. And I did try to soften the blow. I got the guy to agree to a bet. If Mitch can get this thing going and finish a race, he'll get some of the money back. That seems fair. I think Matt is going to be proud."

My mom drew a huge breath. "Parenting without him is tough. I can't wait until his work up north is finished and he can come home." She looked at me and sighed again. "I guess I see your point, Jamie. But Mitch needs that laptop for high school. Now all the money he's saved for it is gone."

"He can earn some of it back when he races. And he's almost fourteen. He can get a job next summer too. I'm sure he'll have enough for a laptop when the time comes."

My mother smiled. "He just turned thirteen two weeks ago! But, yes, he can get a job next summer and put away *every cent*." She emphasized the last two words as she looked at me hard.

"Okay, I get it," I said. "Maybe this was a dumb decision." I ran my hand down the seat of the dirt bike. "But isn't it cool?" I couldn't keep the pride out of my voice.

"Yes, it's cool," Mom agreed. She'd used the same voice when I was little and showed her the creations I'd made. "But you guys better get to work!" She went back into the house.

"Well, that went better than I expected," said Uncle Jamie, wiping the sweat from his forehead. "Jeez, Mitch, you could have warned me. I'd rather stick my head in a hornet's nest!"

"She'll be okay," I said. "After I talk to Dad, he'll get her to see what a great idea this was."

"Hold on a second. I never said this was a great idea." Uncle Jamie began rummaging for tools. "This is going to take some serious work and planning. And I honestly don't know if we're going to be able to get this bike running again."

"Maybe you just need a little help from your friends." Darren and Kelsey were coming up the driveway.

"Hey, I'm Kelsey," Kelsey said to me as they stepped into the garage.

"Hi, I'm Mitchell, er, Mitch." I stumbled over my words and felt my face going red.

"Nice bike. Looks a bit familiar."

"It was Logan's," Darren said.

"I know, doofus," said Kelsey. "The number plate with his last name on it is kind of a giveaway. It's in pretty rough shape. He had work he needed to do on it even before he crashed."

"He did?" I asked.

"Yeah, the suspension needed to be redone, and the pipe was all dented. He said at the last race he was going to do it, but he didn't have the money."

Uncle Jamie looked at Darren. "If he didn't have the suspension done, could that have been the reason why he crashed?"

Darren shrugged. "Hard to say. Would have contributed though, for sure."

"That guy!" Uncle Jamie spat the words. "He's even more of a con artist than I thought. If the bike needed a couple thousand dollars' worth of work before he even crashed it, no wonder he wanted to sell it. And now we have to try and put it all back together."

"I have two old bikes in the barn that are KTM 250s," Kelsey said. "My brother rode one, and the other was mine from my sponsor, but they're pretty trashed. We just kept them for parts. There might be something we can use to get this bike rolling again."

I stared at her. She didn't even know me, and she was willing to give up parts for me? Parts she could maybe use on her own bike if something broke? Wow.

Kelsey seemed to read my thoughts. "It's no big deal." She shrugged. "If I was in your spot, I'd want all the help I could get." She smiled. "And it's so you can race. Racing is everything, so I get it. I want you on those two wheels and out in the dirt."

"The thing is, I'm not very good," I muttered.

"No one is when they start out. You get good by doing it. Which you can't unless you have a bike," Kelsey said. "Which also means you need parts. So just say thanks, and let's have a look at what you're going to need."

"Thanks," I said. I could feel my face turning red again.

Kelsey knelt down to get a better look. "I know for sure I don't have a pipe that isn't all dented up. You might have to buy one of those," she said. "You're going to need new plastic and grips. And these handlebars are completely warped."

"You know, I'm pretty sure I can get you a new pipe and plastic at cost through the shop," Darren said.

"You don't have to do that, man," Uncle Jamie said.

"I want to. I spend summers teaching kids how to ride at training camps, trying to get them into the sport, get them out there riding. Helping Mitch get this bike going is no different. If I can get a few parts, it's no big deal."

"Well, thanks," Uncle Jamie said. "We really appreciate all the help, guys."

Darren joined Kelsey in taking a closer look at the bike. "We need to make a list of everything that needs to be done."

I found some notepaper and a pencil on my dad's workbench and an old car manual to write on. "Okay, I'm ready."

"All right. So plastic, grips and pipe. Put down new for those. But we can probably get handlebars off one of Kelsey's bikes."

"I think I have new plastic at home that doesn't fit my new bike. If it fits Mitch's, he can have it," Kelsey said.

"New graphics for the plastic, but we might be able to cut out our own from standard sheets and just order the numbers," Darren said. "It's tricky, but we can see."

I scribbled down their ideas. I knew they meant the plastic covers that go over the engine in front of the seat. They come in different colors—stock plastic for KTM is orange, for instance. Suzuki is yellow, Yamaha is blue, Honda is red, and Kawasaki is green. You can also get plain white and do custom stickers for the plastic and make the bike look totally different from anything you can buy in the store.

The list continued to grow. They called out names of parts. I had no idea what they were, but I wrote everything down. When the paper was almost full, Darren finally stood up. "I think that's it," he said.

"That's a lot," Kelsey said, checking my list.

"Well, here's hoping we can get most of these parts used," Uncle Jamie said.

Darren stripped off his jacket and rolled up his sleeves.

"What are you doing?" Uncle Jamie asked.

"Helping you pull this bike apart. We'll need to strip it right down to the frame to see what we're dealing with. Might as well get to work."

I groaned as I crawled up the stairs. Every inch of exposed skin was covered in grease and dirt, and my head was crammed full of dirt-bike mechanics. I felt as though I'd spent the last four hours studying for a math final. A hot shower was going to feel good.

"Mitch, can you come down for a second?" Uncle Jamie yelled from the kitchen.

At this point, I was wondering why I had ever thought buying a cheap-but-wrecked dirt bike was a good idea. It would probably have been easier to earn the money to buy a new one by working 24-hour shifts at the local convenience store.

I turned and thumped back down the stairs. "Yeah?"

"Good news. Darren just called. He and Kelsey are coming back tomorrow with a bunch of stuff from Kelsey's old bikes."

"That's great!" I managed a tired smile. "Will it be easier putting everything back together?"

"Oh no," Uncle Jamie said. "Taking it apart was the easy part."

If I could have fainted, I would have.

Chapter Five

Uncle Jamie, Darren and Kelsey were outside my garage before I'd even finished breakfast the next morning. I pulled on a hoodie and went outside with a piece of toast still in my hand.

"Hey, Mitch," Uncle Jamie said. "Is your mom up? I was hoping for a coffee."

"She's already gone to work, but you can help yourself," I said.

"Awesome. Darren, you want one before we get started?"

"Sure!" The two of them ducked into the house.

"You guys must have been on the road before dawn," I said.

"My parents are farmers," Kelsey said. "We always get up early."

"What about Darren?" I asked.

"He's used to it too. He gets to the shop in Lethbridge way before it opens, and sometimes he goes for a practice ride early in the morning."

"It's nice of both of you to help us," I said. I kept my gaze on my feet.

"It's no big deal. Darren spends a lot of time helping kids. He helps my brother and me at races if something breaks on our bikes. My mom could do it, but she's one of the organizers, so she's usually really busy at the races."

"My mom wouldn't know how to fix *anything*," I said. "It was my dad who always did stuff on our bikes."

"My dad fixes the bikes too, but if we're in the middle of seeding or harvesting, he can't leave the farm. They both used to race. My mom has all her trophies in the loft in one of our barns. But Darren is better at working on bikes than both of them, because he does it all the time at the bike shop." She reached into the back of the truck. "I brought the plastic. Let's see if it will fit."

The plastic was plain white. We compared it to the cracked, broken orange plastic on the bike.

"It's pretty close. I think it might work," Kelsey said. "We brought some scraps of sticker paper too. We could design some racing stripes or whatever you want. You could start cutting them out for when the bike is finished."

"That sounds great." I couldn't wait.

Uncle Jamie appeared with a steaming mug in his hand. "I wouldn't start that just yet," he said. "We have a lot to do before we worry about graphics."

Darren followed him out. "We can order numbers for him pretty cheap online. Kelsey can show Mitch later, and he can pick out what he wants. It takes about three weeks for them to come in the mail, so we should do it today."

"First let's see what we have for parts," Uncle Jamie said.

"We brought the parts we thought you could use, and I got a new tailpipe from the shop. I'm just hoping this frame isn't too bad. It's a huge fix if we have to replace that," Darren said.

Uncle Jamie began pulling parts from the back of the truck and laying them out carefully on the garage floor. "We have to rebuild the engine and do the suspension. Those seals are going to be shot."

"I brought the stuff for that. And we got a front fork from Kelsey's."

"Here." Uncle Jamie turned to me. "You can start by washing the air filter. It's going to take Darren and me a few minutes to get organized out here."

"There's some filter cleaner in the back seat," Darren told Kelsey. "You can use that up. It's a bit safer than kerosene," he added.

"Still stinks though," Kelsey said. "Come on, Mitch. I'll show you what to do."

She grabbed an empty bucket and took it down to the end of the driveway and then climbed into the back of Darren's truck. She emerged with a bottle of blue liquid.

"Come on, Mitch," she called. "Bring the air filter."

I looked around, but nothing I saw scattered around the garage looked like a filter. When my dad and I used to ride together, he'd done most of the work on the bikes. I'd watched sometimes, but mostly I'd goofed around while he worked.

Kelsey watched me, then marched back up the driveway. "This thing," she said, picking up what looked like a filthy baseball cap without a brim.

"Oh," I said lamely.

She smiled. "You don't know very much about this stuff, do you?"

"Not really," I admitted. "My dad and I used to go riding together. And then he started having to go away for work a lot, and I outgrew my bike, so we kind of stopped."

"That's okay. You'll learn." Kelsey led me back to the bucket. "So this is easy.

You just drop it in and swish it around for a bit. Then you squeeze out the cleaner and swish it again, until most of the dirt and crud gets loosened or washed out. Then you rinse it in the sink with warm water."

"Oh, my mom is going to love that," I said, catching a whiff of the cleaner. It reminded me of engines, sort of an oil or gasoline smell. It was going to stink up the whole bathroom.

Kelsey handed me some rubber gloves. "Go ahead. Give it a try."

I pulled on the gloves. "Do I really have to wear these?"

"Some guys don't bother, but you're supposed to. That cleaner is a chemical. Not good for you," Kelsey said.

I picked up the sponge baseball cap and gently swirled it in the bucket of cleaner.

"No, put some effort into it," Kelsey said.

I swished harder.

"Excellent," said Kelsey. "Now squeeze it out and do it again!"

I made a face at her. "Look, I know you're trying to be helpful, but I think I have the hang of it now."

"Good. Keep going."

After I'd swished and squeezed for about ten minutes, Kelsey pronounced the filter done. "Okay, go rinse it, and then we can put it in the sun to dry," she said. "Fill the sink with warm water, rinse the whole thing, twist out the water and do it again," she said. "I'll wait here."

I used the sink in the small bathroom by the garage. Amazingly, the dirt from the filter rinsed right out, leaving the sponge looking almost new. I drained the water and took the filter back out to Kelsey to inspect.

"That looks great. One less thing you have to buy." She laid it out on the warm concrete.

I picked up the bucket and started to tip it into the gutter.

"No, stop!" Kelsey cried.

I looked at her in mid-tip.

"You can't dump that stuff down the sewer! It's bad for the environment. We have to put it in a container and take it to the fire hall, where they'll get rid of it properly."

"That seems like a lot of work for just a bit of dirty blue stuff," I said.

"Your uncle and Darren are going to have a bunch of dirty oil and gasoline and other stuff to take over there before this bike is ready to ride."

"Is it really that big of a deal?" I asked.

"Well, I work on our farm. I know what will happen if our water gets polluted. So yeah, I think it's a big deal."

"All right. I get it," I said. I put the bucket back in the garage.

Uncle Jamie and Darren were deep into their work. Uncle Jamie was on his back, trying to unscrew something underneath while Darren held the bike steady.

"Does your dad know yet that you bought this bike?" Kelsey asked as we watched them.

"No. I haven't told him."

"Why don't we call him? I bet he'll be excited for you."

"Well...it's still early. He might be around."

"Then call him!"

I still hesitated. I missed my dad so much that sometimes talking to him made it worse. He'd been texting me all week, asking me to call just to say hi, but I hadn't yet.

I pulled my cell phone out of my pocket. I hit *Dad* in the contact list and waited for it to dial.

"Hey, Dad," I said when he picked up.

"Mitch! Buddy! I've been hoping you would call. I tried you twice yesterday," Dad said.

"Yeah, Uncle Jamie and I were at the race at the track."

"Awesome! Did you guys have fun?"

"Yeah, it was cool. One guy crashed and ate it pretty hard," I said.

"Was he okay?"

"Yeah, but his bike was pretty messed up. I...uh...ended up buying it off him."

"What? Did you say you bought the guy's dirt bike?" asked Dad.

"Yeah, right there on the track. He said he wanted to sell it, and I know it needs

43

work, but I really miss riding with you." The last words came out in a rush.

There was a silence on the end of the phone. "I really miss riding with you too, Bud. I only have two months left here on this contract and then I can come home. How much work does it need?"

I told him everything—how much I'd paid, the bet, the parts Kelsey and Darren were helping us with...all of it. When I was done, Dad asked if he could talk to Uncle Jamie.

When they finished talking, I got back on the phone.

"Sounds like you've got a big project on your hands," Dad said. "But Jamie says he'll help you get it running. And when I get home, you and I can go for a ride together. I'd really look forward to that."

"Me too," I said.

"Do some cool graphics and send me pictures. I want to see this bike in progress, okay?" Dad said.

"Okay."

"Call me whenever you want, Mitch."

"I will. Bye, Dad." As I hit the red dot on my phone, I noticed that Kelsey was watching me closely. "Hey," I said to her, trying to pretend I wasn't feeling sad. "Let's get back to work!"

Chapter Six

"All right. Now you're going to have to kick it harder than normal until we get the choke adjusted," Uncle Jamie said.

I straddled the dirt bike. I found it awkward to move in the heavy boots and riding pants. It had been a long time since I'd worn gear for dirt biking, and I'd grown a lot. Plus, the boots were hand-me-downs from Kelsey's brother, and they were worn out and about two sizes too big.

I lifted my right foot and used my toe to pluck the kick-starter away from the frame.

I settled the arch of my foot over the starter and slammed my leg downward. The bike made a groaning noise and died.

"Do it again," Uncle Jamie said.

I tried again. And again. And...again.

The bike coughed and farted, and finally Uncle Jamie took over. He gave the starter a quick, sharp downward stroke, and the bike sputtered to life. He twisted the throttle, forcing the bike to roar and belch out black smoke.

"It still needs some work," Uncle Jamie said, "but it's running. Give it a test run, and let's see how you do."

I felt my cheeks getting red as I pulled on my helmet. Other riders had watched this performance and were now paying attention to me on my crappy bike. I wished we had test-run the bike out in the woods, not on a public track.

I swung my leg over the seat and settled myself in place. I put one gloved hand on the throttle, the other on the clutch. I squeezed the handle to bring in the clutch, used my foot to take the bike out of neutral and into first gear and gently twisted the throttle to get the bike going.

It lurched forward. Worried that I was going to stall it, and Uncle Jamie and I would have to go through the whole starting process again in front of everybody, I hit the throttle harder. But when the bike shot forward I panicked and squeezed the front brake but forgot to release the throttle. The bike whined and the back tire whirled behind me, kicking up a volcano of dirt. The bike spun out, rotating in circle. It dumped me in the dust before it coughed and died again.

The back tire continued to spin as the bike lay on its side. I felt my face burning as I scrambled to my feet.

Kelsey stepped forward and picked it up. "You whiskey-gripped it," she said matter-of-factly.

I dusted myself off to disguise my shaking nerves. "What?" I said.

"That's when you hit the brake and the throttle at the same time and the back tire spins out because you have the front brake locked," she explained. "The throttle is a bit touchy on this bike. You have to keep your thumb from pressing down on it when you're trying to pull in the front brake."

"Oh," I said.

"Try it again," she said, holding the bike for me to get on.

"Hang on a minute," I said, glancing around.

"Nobody cares," she said. "Everybody whiskey-grips when they're first learning a bike with a clutch. It's okay."

"Easy for you to say," I muttered. My face was still warm, and my palms were wet inside my gloves. I felt like I was taking my life in my hands, getting on this uncontrollable machine. I wished I had my nice, reliable 65 cc bike back. "You probably rode a clutch bike when you were like, two."

"Almost." Kelsey grinned. "Don't be such a chicken. Every single one of these guys out here has dumped their bike more times that they can remember."

"But I'm the guy doing it today," I said.

"Get back on that bike," she said firmly.

"You're never going to be able to race if you can't get the bike out of first gear."

"Okay, okay." I swung my leg back over the seat. This had seemed like such an awesome idea three weeks ago.

I kicked at the starter. This time the engine came to life immediately. I revved the throttle with more confidence than I felt and slowly let go of the clutch. The bike hiccuped, and I started moving forward.

"That's it!" yelled Kelsey. "Keep going, Mitch!"

My mouth felt dry. I pushed the throttle a bit harder, squeezed the clutch. The bike kicked smoothly into second gear, and the next thing I knew, I was riding around the track. Mind you, it was the kids' track, but still. I was actually riding! The bike actually worked!

On my second lap the bike started making an odd grinding noise. I braked as I came around to Kelsey and Uncle Jamie.

"That doesn't sound good," Uncle Jamie said. "We need to check a few things. I think we have to adjust the choke, for one."

I got off and grabbed my water bottle while Kelsey, Uncle Jamie and Darren busied themselves around the bike. I tried to steady my nerves. I knew how to ride, but this felt a lot different than when my dad and I had gone out together in the woods. I felt like everyone was watching. It was embarrassing, because I knew I wasn't that good.

Uncle Jamie fired up the bike again. The engine roared to life, belching out a plume of smoky exhaust before settling into a confident hum. "Come on, Mitch!" he called. "Give it another try!"

I swung my leg over the seat. I remembered what I had to do, and the bike and I took off.

Kelsey cheered. I pushed the bike a bit harder. It felt like I was rocketing around the track.

"Hey, slow down!" a dad yelled after me. "There are little kids on this track! Racers like you belong on the big track."

He couldn't have said anything else that would have made me feel more awesome.

Chapter Seven

"That was amazing!" Kelsey said as I pulled the bike up beside her. "You did great!"

I undid the straps on my helmet and tugged it off. "Wow. I can't believe it works." The smile just wouldn't come off my face. "It actually really works!"

"I know." Kelsey laughed. "It's a miracle!"

"Where's Uncle Jamie?"

"Darren called. He's picking me up, but Jamie wanted to meet him at the shop for some part or something, so they went over there."

"Oh, okay." Macleod Motosports is right across the street. They also own the track, so when someone breaks something on their bike, the shop is right there. Talk about smart business.

"I'm going to go get something to drink from the store," said Kelsey. "You want anything?"

"No, I'm good." I took off my gloves as she walked away and began examining the radiator, pretending I actually knew what I was doing. Really, I was just waiting for Uncle Jamie to come back.

"Hey!" said a voice behind me. "Nice bike."

I turned. It was Logan, the rider who had sold me the dirt bike. "Hi," I said. I didn't know what else to say. Thanks, maybe? But I didn't think he was really complimenting the bike. I waited.

"Yeah, looks real good. I think maybe you got too good of a deal on it," Logan said.

"I think two thousand bucks for a pile of junk was more than fair," I countered. "It wasn't even worth that."

"Looks like it's worth it now. All you need are some fancy graphics and a few wins, and you could get a sponsor," Logan said.

What was this guy getting at? I shook my head. "Listen, I'm pretty new at this whole thing, but a deal's a deal. I paid you way too much money in the first place." My words surprised me, but I kept going. "We had to put a lot of work and parts into getting this thing running again. So why don't you either back off or tell me what's on your mind."

Logan stepped forward, putting his face close to mine. "I'll tell you what's on my mind. I don't like some dorky little kid taking advantage of a bad situation. I crashed hard that day. You stepped up and offered me a deal I couldn't refuse. Now you've got a bike that's worth about five thousand dollars after paying only two. You call that a fair deal?"

"Yeah, I do. The bike was ready for the scrap heap. My uncle said even a thousand bucks was too much. So, yeah, I do think it's a fair deal."

"Well, I don't," said Logan, still in my face.

"Well, that's too bad." I was not backing down.

"For you. Because what do you think is going to happen if the story about this little bet gets out? Who do you think people are going to support? A rider who's been in the series for years or some nobody?"

"What does that have to do with anything?"

"Maybe nothing, but people might not be so friendly when you show up to the races."

"Sounds to me like you're scared you're going to lose the bet and owe me a thousand bucks," I said coolly. Wow, I sounded way braver than I felt. My knees felt like they were going to give out.

Logan clenched his jaw. "I'm not scared of anything, let alone a runt like you. You couldn't win a race even on the best bike money can buy."

"Oh yeah?"

"Yeah!"

"If that last race is an example, it's no wonder your nickname is Crash." I had no idea if Logan had a nickname. I had just made that up. But it seemed to hit a nerve, because his face turned red.

"You've got a pretty big mouth, kid. Let's see you stand behind it. I think that bike should be mine. I think you paid way less than it is worth. The bet was that if you could finish a race on it, I'd have to pay you back half of your money. I think it's obvious you can finish a race on it, so maybe we should up the bet a little. Whoever places the highest in their class in the next race gets to keep the bike."

"What? That isn't fair! I haven't even raced before, and I paid you for this bike!"

"Yeah, if I win, I'll give you half your money back and keep the bike. If you win, you still get half your money back *and* keep the bike. A much better deal for you, I'd say."

I thought about it for a moment. "No," I said, shaking my head.

"Scared?" Logan grinned slyly.

"No, it's just that we've put a lot of money and effort into this bike now. There's no way I'll risk losing it. And I wouldn't be getting a better deal. If I finish a race, I'm getting half my money back anyway."

"I think I see some of the race organizers over there. Maybe I should tell them the extent of my injuries that day...that I had a concussion and was not thinking clearly. And now some kid is trying to swindle me. I think that might even be illegal. Maybe I should check with the police."

I swallowed. Was it illegal? Uncle Jamie would have known if it were. He wouldn't have done anything wrong. But then, none of us had thought Logan was badly hurt that day. Maybe he *did* have a concussion though...

"If they find out, they'll just take the bike away from you anyway," Logan pressed on. "I'm giving you a chance to keep it. All you have to do is place higher than I do in your class. And what are you going to ride, Beginner Pee Wee? You could beat the five-year-olds easy."

I gritted my teeth.

"At least if the story comes out, your uncle will take the fall as the con man. You're still too young to go to jail."

I didn't know how much of what Logan was saying was true, but I couldn't risk Uncle Jamie getting into trouble because of me. He'd worked so hard on this bike for me. The least I could do was win a race for him. I reached my hand out slowly.

"You've got a deal." I shook Logan's hand.

Chapter Eight

"Give it some gas!" Uncle Jamie shouted over the roar of the throttle. "Rev it!"

Clouds of blue smoke erupted from the exhaust pipe. Then the engine settled into a comfortable rumble.

Uncle Jamie pulled on his helmet. "It's running a bit rich, but I'll adjust it when we get back. It should be okay for a practice ride." He threw his leg over his own bike. "Ready?"

I nodded.

Kelsey and Darren were already heading down the path. They rode slowly, so I could figure out what I was doing.

"Stay in first until we get down past the creek," Uncle Jamie called out. "Then shift to second gear once we have a bit more space."

"Okay!" I yelled back.

I trailed behind them, bumping carefully over the rocks and roots, easing the bike down the narrow path. I was very aware of the thick trees lining the route. I hoped I wouldn't whiskey-grip the throttle again and run into one.

We got down to the bottom, rode along the creek and crossed over a wooden bridge. We crossed a meadow, and right ahead was a hill. It wasn't so big, but because I had to climb it on my bike, it looked like a mountain.

Kelsey hit the throttle on her bike and buzzed right up it, easily making her way over rocks and around shrubs. Darren followed her, but Uncle Jamie glanced back. I swallowed against the lump of fear in my throat and gave him a thumbs-up. He nodded and increased his speed to take the hill.

I exhaled and gave the bike more gas. The engine began to whine, and I shifted up to second, which immediately gave me more speed. More than I was ready for. The back end seesawed a bit as I tried to get control, and I weaved into the grass. I clenched my teeth and tried to remember everything I used to do with my dad. I stood up on the pegs and leaned into the bike until I had it back on the path, then lowered my butt and gunned it. The bike flew, and I eased up on the gas as I crested the hill. My hands were shaking so bad, I had to stop. The other three were navigating a flatter stretch on top but they weren't far ahead. Elation and adrenaline raced through my veins. I had done it, really done it. I'd ridden the bike harder than ever before and actually controlled it, instead of it controlling me. Maybe we hadn't reached a full understanding yet that I was the one in charge, but my dirt bike knew I was the boss.

I think.

Kelsey circled back. "What are you waiting for?" she cried. "Let's go!"

I took another deep breath and kicked the bike out of neutral and back into first gear. "Okay, let's do it!"

I was dirty and sweaty and felt like I had been beaten with a big stick for hours. Every muscle was tense and aching. I had refused to ask for a break, but I badly needed one now. I accelerated until I was close to Uncle Jamie and waved like a maniac until he looked at me. I gave him a thumbs-down and halted my bike.

He immediately slowed down and cut the motor. "What's the matter?"

"I need to stop." I crawled off the seat and fell into a damp clump of tall grass. "I need a break."

"You did pretty good. We've been riding for an hour."

"An hour!" I croaked. "I thought we'd been out here for at least five!"

"No." Uncle Jamie shook his head. "The races typically last for about two hours, so this is the halfway point."

"Oh my gosh." I rolled onto my back and stared up at the sky. "There's no way I can do this for two hours. I'm dying." Clouds floated across the clear blue sky above me, and the fresh smell of the grass filled my nose. I could lie here until tomorrow, I thought. Maybe then I could get up.

"You're not dying," Uncle Jamie said. "You're just not used to riding. Kelsey and I will break you in gently."

"This isn't gentle—this is torture."

"Stop being such a wuss." Uncle Jamie grabbed my hand and pulled me up. Kelsey and Darren had circled back. Kelsey braked hard as she came up to me, swinging the bike's back end in a circle just for fun.

"Show-off," I muttered. How did she still have so much energy?

"Come on, Mitch! The best part of the trail is just ahead. We get to go down the cliffs."

"*What?*"

"They're not really cliffs," Darren said. "Kelsey's exaggerating. They're the bluffs that lead back down toward the creek at this end. Some of them are steep, but most aren't too bad."

I looked at Uncle Jamie. I didn't want to admit it, but I didn't think I could do it. My arms were on fire already.

Uncle Jamie hesitated. "Is there another route that's a bit easier? I think Mitch has just about had enough for his first time out."

Darren shook his head. "I don't know. The race trails always lead down there at some point. We could follow the ridge and just see where it takes us."

"Let's try it." Uncle Jamie pulled his goggles back over his eyes and kicked the starter. I started my bike and followed Kelsey and Darren.

The high, grassy peak gave way to trees and hills, and some of the route was actually fun to ride. I stopped being so scared and just enjoyed the swoop of the bike as it took the dips and turns of the trail. The break in the grass had helped, and I was beginning to think I would make it back to camp without a rescue helicopter.

"Where's the creek from here?" Kelsey asked when we pulled up together to get our bearings.

"I have no idea," Darren said. "I know this area pretty well, but I've never been this way. The creek should be to the west, so let's head in that general direction. Once we cross the creek, the gravel road shouldn't be far off. We can ride that back if we have to."

We carried on. Until we hit a barbed-wire fence.

"Now what?" Kelsey said, clearly frustrated by the stops and starts.

"Well, there's no going through this," Darren answered.

"Why not? There's probably a gap in the fence somewhere," I said.

"For one thing, it's private land. That's why there's a fence," Kelsey said. "For another, they definitely don't want anyone on their land. Look at that." She pointed down the fence line.

I eased my bike along the fence until I got close enough for a good look.

Signs. Some were small, some were big.

No Trespassing. Violators will be prosecuted.

Keep out.

Responsible government protects the environment.

One was huge with red letters. It said *Sour Gas,* with a circle around the words and a line through it.

"There's more down there." Kelsey gestured at the fence.

We rode a short distance alongside it. Every twenty yards or so, there was another batch of threatening signs.

"Friendly," I said.

"Yeah." Kelsey frowned. "I think we better get away from here. Let's tell Darren." She turned her bike around and putted back to the two men.

I took a last look at the signs before I followed her. *Friendly* was definitely the wrong word. Something about the way the messages were scrawled had sent a chill right through me.

Chapter Nine

This was it. Race day. The day of the bet. The day I might have to give up my bike. If I lost. Which I didn't plan on. Logan could kiss my hairy butt. I was keeping my bike.

I watched the Intermediate Men's class lined up at the mark. There were so many racers, they stretched the full length of the field. Kelsey was in there somewhere, and so was Logan. I squinted into the sunshine, looking for Kelsey's gear. At the last race she had worn gray and black, and it had been hard to pick her out. This time I knew she had on bright lime-green and orange. I spotted her before I saw her bike number. Logan I still hadn't spotted. I looked for his number and eventually found him on the far edge in red-and-blue gear.

I was racing in the Intermediate Kids' class. Uncle Jamie had tried to get me to do Beginner Kids, but that was just way too embarrassing. I might technically be a beginner, but I didn't want to race with nine-year-olds who had just moved up from Expert Pee Wee. Especially if they beat me. Jeez, talk about humiliating. No, Intermediate Kids was better. Those guys were all around twelve to sixteen years old, so I wouldn't feel like a complete idiot racing with them. There was, however, a really solid chance I was going to come in last. And potentially lose the bet.

I pushed that thought out of my mind. The Pee Wee races had already started on the other side of the road. I had just enough time to watch Kelsey's and Logan's start before I had to get ready for my own race.

My stomach churned, and I had to swallow hard against the nerves.

The guy starting the race yelled something, waving his flag to get the racers' attention, but I couldn't hear over the noise of the bike engines. The racers must have heard, though, because they all cut their engines and placed their hands on top of their helmets. A tense silence fell.

The race starter waved the flag in a quick downward swoop, and the racers sprang into action, cranking throttles and kick-starting the bikes. A buzzing roar filled the silence, and the first riders off the mark spun through the dust on the trail, up the grassy slope past where I was standing with the other spectators. Kelsey was among the first, Logan not far behind. Within seconds, all the riders had disappeared over the crest of the hill, leaving only clouds of dust and a faint buzzing behind.

I turned and headed back to my uncle's trailer. In a maze of campers and trucks, I found our tiny tent trailer with my bike parked beside it.

"Ready to go?" Uncle Jamie asked. I nodded, feeling my stomach knot. I pulled my helmet on and started the bike, feeling more and more uneasy. Who was I kidding? I didn't know how to race. I barely knew how to ride.

"The kids' start is across the road on the other side. You'll join up for part of the west side of the men's loop, but not all of it, so watch for the colored ribbons. They'll tell you at the start."

I nodded. We had already discussed all this. Uncle Jamie clapped my shoulder. "Good luck, Mitch!"

I had begun to pull away from the trailer when a wave of nausea hit me so hard I didn't even have time to react. I threw up, right in my helmet. I yanked desperately on the clasp under my chin and ripped it off, depositing the rest of my breakfast into the grass beside my bike.

"Oh, great." I closed my eyes. I was pretty sure this was not the best way to start a race.

"Not to worry. I'll rinse it out. Your dad puked in his helmet before just about every race."

I opened one eye. "Really?"

"Well, maybe not every race. But at least four or five of them. Something of a family tradition, I guess. Wait until we tell him!"

I handed Uncle Jamie my helmet. He wiped it out with paper towels, doused it with disinfectant, rinsed it and blotted it dry with an old towel.

"Good as new," he said, handing it back to me.

I frowned. "Don't we have a spare helmet?"

"Just mine, and it's too big. Besides, this has your bar code on it, and the race starts in ten minutes, so there's not enough time to get another one registered."

"Right." The bar codes were stuck on the side of the helmets, and as racers went through the checkpoints, volunteers scanned the codes to keep track of how many laps a racer had completed and where they had placed.

I pulled the damp helmet back on. It smelled strongly of pine trees and faintly of vomit. With my stomach now empty and my nerves completely shot, I kicked my bike starter and roared up and over the road with way more confidence than I felt.

I pulled into the group of Intermediate Kids racers. The Expert Kids class was just getting briefed on the rules of the start. I didn't know anyone in my class. I didn't know anyone here, period. The only reason I knew I was in the right place was because Kelsey had brought me to this spot the night before and walked me through what to expect.

The Expert Kids lined up. The announcer didn't have a fancy microphone or anything, so he had to yell at the top of his lungs.

My head was buzzing, and I didn't even hear what he said. I just saw the scramble of dirt bikes fighting to be first down the trail. As their dust settled, the Intermediate Kids lined up. Everyone revved their engines. The noise vibrated in the trees. We put our bikes into neutral. I gave silent thanks that it wasn't a dead start. The flag rose, and the next pause seemed to last forever. I could feel my heart beating, throbbing in my temples, and I held my breath.

The flag swooped toward the ground. All of us fumbled to get our bikes into first gear. The first kids spun off in a cloud of dust, and the rest got their wheels under them and made respectable exits. I sputtered off the start, gave the engine gas without remembering the clutch and panicked. I let go of both the throttle and the clutch and promptly stalled the bike. Palms sweating and wanting to die of embarrassment, I toed out the starter and tried to kick-start it. Nothing.

I tried again.

And again.

And again.

Uncle Jamie and a couple of dads came over and motioned me to get off. They really hammered at the starter, and finally the bike burst into life.

"Go!" Uncle Jamie pointed down the

path. I leaped onto the seat and carefully put the bike into first before bumping down the trail.

I didn't want to make any more mistakes. Stalling the bike had already cost me a lot of time. If I placed last, Logan would win back the bike for sure.

I wound my way through the trees, keeping a careful eye on the pink ribbons tied at intervals along the trail. If Uncle Jamie hadn't explained the rules to me the day before, I'd have been sunk. I was so nervous at the start, I didn't hear anything race officials told us. The pink ribbons mark the trail. You have to follow them. When pink and blue ribbons are tied together, that means the trail branches off, and the ribbons show you which turn to take. Yellow ribbons warn of risky things ahead, like a road, a cliff, a hole or some other hazard.

I followed the pink ribbons, gained momentum and pushed the bike harder. I stood on the pegs and did my best to make my way around roots and rocks and dips in the trail. It was hard to keep an eye on the ground in front of me and still watch for the ribbons, but after a while I worked out a system. I watched for ribbons from the corner of my eye and kept a close watch on the trail. Then I hit a section of roots. It took all my concentration to keep the bike from slipping. When I got through it, I hit the throttle and blasted through a flat stretch. When I hit the next patch of bush, I finally looked up. There wasn't a pink ribbon anywhere.

I was lost.

Chapter Ten

Cursing, I turned the bike around. I had no idea when I'd lost the trail, but this was going to cost me more time. I backtracked carefully, the way Kelsey had told me to if I ever got off course, making sure I followed my tracks exactly.

Back at the root section, I found a pink and blue ribbon tied together. I'd been so busy watching the trail, I'd missed this marker. Luckily, I made it back to the course without much trouble. Kelsey had told me about races where she had been off course for ages before she could find her way back.

I had a lot of time to make up. If I didn't pick up the pace, it was going to cost me my dirt bike. But I couldn't afford to get off course again. I had no choice but to slow down, take the easier lines, watch for the ribbons. Be smart. Stay safe. If I crashed or lost my way, I would be even worse off.

So I rode. Rode up hills, around trees, down gullies. I rode through bushes and dead grass so thick I could hardly see the trail. I rode until my hands ached. My butt was killing me from chafing against the seat. I'd have given a million dollars for a tub of baby-butt cream.

I still rode. Faster when I could. After what seemed like forever, I heard the faint noise of other bike engines. I was no longer alone in the woods.

I couldn't see anyone yet, but the noise made me feel better. I continued along the pink-ribbon pathway. I stood on the pegs. My rear end was so sore, I had to get some relief. But it had become kind of fun, weaving along the trail. The air was fresh and crisp, the sun bright. I'd stopped worrying about the race at least a little bit. Maybe a person can only take so much adrenaline-related stress before the brain shuts down for a while.

I kind of floated around some trees into an area thick with green bushes. Low bushes with berries hanging from them. I slowed, and as I did, three little brown furry things popped out onto the trail.

Those are bears, my tired brain thought. Bear cubs.

Suddenly the fatigue disappeared, and my brain was shouting at me. *Those are bears!* Brown bear cubs! Oh my god, they could be grizzlies. And where there are cubs, there is usually a mother.

My instinct was to drive the bike straight into the bushes away from the cubs. But what if the mother was in there? And what if the bike stalled if I got on rough terrain in there and I couldn't manage it?

I fought my instant panic and skirted gently around the cubs on the trail, then gunned it as soon as I was past. I didn't dare risk a look back, but I hoped the screeching whine of the engine as I pushed it hard instead of shifting would scare the cubs right back into the bush, and the mother too.

I was shocked they were out here. Given the constant hum of motorcycle engines, I had thought wildlife would get as far away as they could.

But then, there isn't much that scares off a grizzly. And cubs wouldn't know any better. They'd probably just wanted more berries.

I'd forgotten all about my sore butt and aching hands. I hammered the throttle and pushed the bike harder and faster than I ever had. I put as much distance between myself and the bear cubs as I could.

When I thought I was safe, I stopped for a quick rest. I stretched out my aching hands and took a sip of water. And it suddenly occurred to me how amazing this all was. Wow! In what other sport would I see baby bears up close?

I got back on my bike and threaded my way through the trees. Eventually I began to pass people on the trail...a few riders down with broken bikes, a couple of racers who were covered in mud, exhausted. I wasn't quite in last place. And I began to hope.

I buzzed up a rocky incline, one I would have been too scared to even try a week earlier. I shocked myself by how easily I took it. Riding suddenly seemed easy. Well, easier. My back tire slid on the loose shale, and I struggled to keep my balance. But I kept going. I sailed along the top of the ridge. The sun and the sky touched me. The air flowed through me, cold and clean. It was a wonderful feeling.

The trail dipped down, winding back into the trees. I watched carefully for the pink ribbons, because I had to pay close attention to the trail on this part. The area had been partially logged, and fallen trees were scattered near the path, among new-growth trees and the remaining old-stand forest. Roots popped up all over the trail, and avoiding them was tricky. My back tire kept slipping, and I had to wrestle the bike around each turn. Sweat trickled down inside my helmet.

I was focusing so hard on the trail that I almost rode past before I saw it. A flash of lime green in the grass beside the trail. And a bike on its side. It took me a moment to register what I was seeing.

Kelsey!

Chapter Eleven

I jumped off my bike, letting it fall against a tree. "Kelsey!" I leaned over her. "Are you okay?"

She didn't answer, but she opened her eyes. I touched her shoulder. "Kelsey?"

She winced in pain. "Don't move me," she gasped.

"What's wrong? What happened?" I asked.

"I crashed," she whispered. "No biggie, but I landed on that stump on my back."

I looked at the tree stump behind us and said a few really bad words. "Can you move?" I tried hard not to panic.

"My arms and my legs," she said, reading my thoughts. "I'm not paralyzed."

I gave silent thanks for that.

"But I've been lying out here for a while. It feels like hours," she said. "No one stopped. I figure the sweepers must be coming soon."

I'd forgotten all about the race. "They should be, unless they're somewhere else on the course."

"There's a bad spot a few miles back. A bunch of guys got stuck getting up a hill in the mud," Kelsey whispered. "They're probably all there."

"I could ride back there to get help," I said.

"It won't help. There's no cell service, so they can't even call 9-1-1," Kelsey said. "And anyway, there's no way to get an ambulance up here."

"What about the emergency helicopter?" I suggested.

"No place for it to land." Kelsey tried to sit up, her breath catching in her throat. She was in too much pain to even cry.

"Be careful." I tried to support her, but she shook her head.

"I think my ribs are broken," she said. Her body was shaking, and her hands were cold. I stripped off my dirty gloves and tried to warm her fingers in my palms.

"I could ride back to the camp. We could get a stretcher and come up on foot."

"That will take hours. It's probably twenty miles back to camp. I can't wait out here that long."

I knew she couldn't. I don't have a lot of medical knowledge, but I know about shock. A person can die from it, and Kelsey was already shaking and pale.

I didn't know what to do. I could wait here with her—eventually someone would come. But each passing minute meant more time without a doctor's help.

"I'm going to ride," Kelsey said.

"What?" I snapped to attention.

"I'm going to ride," she said again.

85

"You can't ride with broken ribs! And you might be bleeding internally—we don't know."

"We can't just stay here," Kelsey said. "I have to get off this mountain or I'm going to die out here." She said this calmly, like she was discussing the weather.

I stared at her. She stared back. "Can you do it?" I asked.

"I don't know. Help me?" She looked terrified. I knew I was.

"Of course. Tell me what to do," I said.

"Help me stand, but don't put any pressure on my body. Just put your arms under my armpits to keep me steady."

Any other time I would have made a joke about deodorant, but this was not the moment. My mouth felt as dry as cotton as I slipped my arms around her. I didn't want to hurt her.

She grunted as she stood, swaying slightly until she got her balance. "I'm okay," she said. I pulled her bike upright. The smell of gas hit me, and I looked at the dark stain on the ground.

"I'm out of fuel," Kelsey said. "I couldn't reach the bike to turn the gas valve off, and it drained out."

Could anything go right for us? I tried to stay calm. "What are we going to do now? I can't double you all the way back. It's too dangerous if your ribs are broken."

"You have to take your tank off and pour some of your gas into my bike," Kelsey said. Her face was gray now. I knew I had to hurry.

"Tell me how," I said.

"Look under the seat and undo the screws so you can take your seat off," she said. "I have tools in the pouch strapped to my bike."

I propped her bike against a tree so I could get the pouch open. I found a screwdriver and a wrench and knelt beneath my bike. I loosened the bolts and pulled off my seat. "Now what?"

"Undo the valve underneath the gas tank. There's a tube there that leads into the carburetor."

I unclipped it and worked the tank loose. I lifted the whole thing off and stepped over to Kelsey's bike. I unscrewed the gas cap, put the tube in and let the gas flow out. Cold sweat trickled down my face, but I couldn't move. I watched the fuel dribble in. When my tank was about half-empty, I set it down.

Kelsey leaned on her bike for support.

"Are you okay?" I asked. We both knew she wasn't, but she nodded anyway.

I twisted her gas cap back on, shoved my tank back on my bike, reclamped the valve and set my seat in place. I stuffed the bolts in the holes, rotated the wrench as fast I could and threw everything back in Kelsey's tool pouch.

"Okay." I took a deep breath. "Ready?"

"Yeah. Let's roll," she said.

Chapter Twelve

I kicked Kelsey's starter and got the bike going, then helped her lift her leg over the seat. She clenched her teeth against the pain, and I tried to avoid squeezing her in any way.

"Good?" I asked when she was settled. She nodded, and I started my own bike. "You go first," I said. "I'll follow you."

Kelsey rolled carefully down the path. The bike bumped over the roots, and she stood up on the pegs. I didn't know how she could handle doing this, but we had no other option. And so we rode.

We neared the ridge where we had done our practice ride. I gunned my bike a little and pulled up beside Kelsey where the path opened up. I motioned for her to stop. "I don't think we should keep going on the course," I shouted. "It's going to be too hard. If we take the trail that we practiced on, it will be a lot shorter."

"If we cut off course, there won't be anyone to help if we go down," Kelsey said.

"Can you honestly ride down the bluffs, through the creek and all that?" I asked, pointing.

"No," Kelsey said.

"Then let's go." I took the trail to the right, away from the pink ribbons that told us where to go. I prayed we wouldn't get lost, that I actually could find my way. The trail wound down the hill gradually, and we skirted the creek until I saw a wooden bridge. We crossed on that—much easier than trying to go through the water—and snaked along the other side. I was beginning to worry that we were going the wrong way, as nothing looked familiar, until those creepy warning signs started appearing.

"This way!" I yelled, pulling up along the barbed-wire fence. I looked back. Kelsey had stopped her bike, her foot braced against a fence post. The trail was too narrow to turn around. I propped up my bike and walked back on foot.

"You okay?"

She shook her head. "I need to stop for a minute."

I looked at Kelsey's face—what I could see of it. The helmet couldn't hide the exhaustion in her eyes. We were running out of time. I had to get her out of here.

"We're not going around," I said, making an instant decision. "We're going through."

"Through what?" Kelsey said, too tired to understand.

"The fence. We're going through the fence. The land here looks pretty flat...there are probably fields on the other side of the trees. It'll be a lot easier for you to ride."

"It's private property," Kelsey said.

"You think I care about that?" I said forcefully. "They can take their private property and shove it. You need help. And we're going to get it."

I yanked open her tool pouch and pulled out a pair of pliers with sharp blades on their jaws. I hoped they were sturdy enough to slash barbed wire.

They weren't, really. But with sheer will and eye-popping strength I didn't know I had, I pressed the blades through each strand of wire until I had a break in the fence. Rain started to spit down as I pulled the wires backward to make an opening. I pushed Kelsey's bike through, then my own. I held the gap for her.

"Come on, Kelsey. You can do it."

She shuffled through. I started her bike and helped her on again.

"Not far," I yelled over the engine noise. She nodded.

I wheeled around a tree and tried to find a path. Luckily the terrain was smoother on this side, likely worn down from cattle, judging by the manure I had just ridden through. I made a mental note to tell someone about the gap in the fence when we got back, so that no cattle escaped.

The bike engines buzzed as we rode through the aspen trees. I kept glancing back. Kelsey had to ride standing up the whole way, but she seemed to be handling it—until it really started to rain.

The cold soaked through my jersey. I didn't know how much farther we had to go. I worried about Kelsey being in shock and whether the cold was making things worse. We had been skirting the fence line, but I broke away to begin the trek through the trees. I could see an old shed up ahead. As the rain pelted us, we pulled up to it. A broken lock dangled from the bracket, so it was easy to pull the door open.

"Come on, let's duck in here for a few minutes. Maybe the rain will lighten up," I said.

"I can't keep stopping," Kelsey said. "We have to keep going."

"You're freezing," I said. "At least get inside for a minute to dry off. Do you have anything besides your jersey?"

"I don't usually race with a suitcase strapped on the back," Kelsey snapped.

I sighed. "I know that. But not even paper towel for wiping your goggles?"

"I usually get that at the checkpoint."

I glanced around the shed to see if there was anything we could use. All I saw were cans of gasoline, a few old lanterns and tools and a pile of thin plywood squares. Looking closer, I saw that the squares were painted in different colors and attached to handles. Protest signs. The one on top said something about the government and sour-gas pipelines. I lifted it and saw another about pollution. I dropped them. They made me uneasy, and I had enough to worry about right now.

"Well, no towels or umbrellas, so this was useless," I tried to joke. I looked outside the door. "The rain isn't coming down as hard, but I don't think it's going to stop. We'll just have to ride through it. Unless you want to stay here while I go get help." I looked at Kelsey. "You could rest, and I could bring someone back. Maybe they could get a vehicle through here."

"And maybe they couldn't," Kelsey said. "We have no idea. And I don't think I can wait for hours alone." She swallowed. "We have to keep going, Mitch."

"I know. It just sucks out there, and I want to make sure you're okay."

"I don't think I'll really be okay until we get out of here."

And to a hospital, I thought, but didn't say out loud. Kelsey looked worse than ever, and I felt terrible watching her push through this. But there was no other choice now. We had to keep going until we found our way out, back to camp, back to Uncle Jamie and Darren and Kelsey's mom and dad. Nothing else mattered.

So again we started off. I veered onto the flattest stretch of grass meadow I could find and headed straight west toward where I thought we'd meet the main road. A few minutes' ride brought us to a trail that turned into a dirt road. This made riding much easier, and we were able to get up a bit more speed. The road was obviously well used, so I wasn't surprised to see barns and sheds and a ranch house when we crested a small hill.

"Look!" I shouted back to Kelsey. "There's a house. The main road will probably be just past it." I debated whether we should stop at the house and ask for help or head straight back to camp.

As we got closer, and just as I had decided we should stop, an elderly woman burst out the back door and onto the porch.

"Get off my land!" she screeched at us. She brandished a big stick. "Get off, you with your filthy machines, tearing up the earth. Get out!"

"But we need help," I said, stopping my bike. "We're sorry, but—"

"I don't care!" she shouted. Wisps of gray hair flew around her face in the wind and rain. "You take those machines right back where you came from and don't ever come back!"

I tried again. "It's an emergency...we need a phone—" But the woman wouldn't listen. She raised her stick. I decided we had to get the heck out of there. Kelsey was already ahead of me, and we tore down the driveway and out onto the dirt road. We waited until we were out of sight before we paused. Kelsey was white and shaking.

"That woman was crazy," she gasped.

"Or just miserable," I said, more angry than scared. "You would think she would have wanted to help." I looked around. "We're almost there. Go. I'll be right behind you."

Kelsey put her bike in gear and looked at me.

"You can do it," I said encouragingly. "It's easy now. Just a little farther."

She roared off down the road, still standing on the pegs. I followed her as closely as I could. We reached the race site minutes later. A few trucks loaded down with trailers and bikes were pulling out. The kids' races must be over, but everyone else was still finishing. It felt like we'd been out there for days.

I pulled into Kelsey's trailer spot, and she was already there, helmet off.

Her dad was unstrapping her boots. I spotted her mom unhitching the trailer from the truck.

"We were pretty worried when you didn't show up at the checkpoint. I knew you had to be down somewhere. We sent the sweepers out after you." Her dad shook his head. "I was just about to drive out and get cell service to call an ambulance."

"We cut course. I had to get back," Kelsey whispered.

"Shouldn't we still call an ambulance?" I said. "She's hurt really bad."

"It'll take them forty-five minutes to get here," Kelsey's mom said, panic in her voice. "It's faster if we take her straight into the hospital in Lethbridge. That's closest." She turned to Darren and Uncle Jamie, who had run up as soon as they spotted us. "Unless you think we need the emergency helicopter?"

Darren looked grim. "Just go. You can call for help on the road if you have to. At least you can use your phone on the highway. But she needs medical attention right away."

Kelsey's mom had the truck and trailer apart within seconds. She turned the truck around and we quickly got Kelsey loaded into the back, lying down across the seat.

She looked at me. "Thank you," she whispered.

I managed a weak grin. "No problem," I said.

"We'll load Kelsey's bike and lock everything up. Don't worry about anything here. And if you need us to, we'll haul the trailer to your place," Uncle Jamie told Kelsey's mom. And then the Murrays were gone in a cloud of dust.

I coughed. "I'm going to take my bike over to our place," I said. "Then I'll come back and help."

Uncle Jamie's eyes watered a bit. "You did a very brave thing, Mitch. I'm really proud of you."

I had to avoid looking at him. My hands started to shake. Now that we were back, the enormity of what had just happened hit me hard. I kicked the starter and wheeled around toward our trailer. But I had a quick detour to make first.

I drove straight to Logan's trailer. It was big and fancy. Lucky for me, it was also empty.

I knew I'd lost the bet. The race had finished long before Kelsey and I had made it back, and I'd never even gotten through a single checkpoint. Logan had won the bike, fair and square. There wasn't one single thing I could do about it.

I cut the bike engine, slid off the seat and walked away.

Chapter Thirteen

Uncle Jamie started the truck. We were packed up and finally ready to pull out. Darren was taking care of the Murrays' trailer.

"Lethbridge is almost an hour's drive," Uncle Jamie said. "We could call Kelsey's mom and see how she's doing."

"No. I want to see her," I said.

Uncle Jamie studied me. "Okay."

I couldn't explain it to him. I'd just worried so much on that mountain about getting Kelsey out okay that I needed to see her to make sure she was actually going to be all right.

"You get everything loaded up okay while I was helping Darren?"

I just nodded. I let Uncle Jamie think I had loaded my bike with his. I had tarped his dirt bike and the gear bags in the back of the truck because of the rain, so it was easy to hide the fact that my dirt bike was not in there too.

The truck swayed and bumped over the uneven ground, towing our little tent trailer along the dirt road, past the empty campsites. Almost everyone else had already gone. The rain had left the meadows soggy and the road a slick line of sticky mud. The truck tires churned against it, grabbing what traction they could until we pulled up onto the gravel road. The going was easier here.

"That's why that lady has all those signs up," Uncle Jamie said.

"Huh?"

"The rancher you told me about, who wouldn't help you and Kelsey. She thinks dirt bikes and trucks and quads and any-thing else with a motor shouldn't be allowed on land like this. That those vehi-cles churn up the earth and ruin it."

"But dirt bikes stay on a single path, like bicycles. They don't damage anything," I protested.

"We say that, but some people see it differently," Uncle Jamie said. "Plus, there's pollution. Some people don't want engines polluting the air."

"They better not own any cars then," I grumbled. I was still furious about that woman not helping us.

"You see my point," said Uncle Jamie. "I'm just trying to figure out why that rancher acted the way she did. She had all those signs on the fence when we did our practice ride. She obviously doesn't want anyone around her property at all."

"Whatever," I said. I didn't feel like talking about it anymore.

Uncle Jamie drove in silence for a while. I stared out the window, too bummed about the loss of my dirt bike and too worried about Kelsey to say anything. In the distance, a heavy plume of smoke billowed into the air.

"What's that?" I said. I opened my window to get a better look. The faint smell of rotten eggs blew in. "Phew!" I wrinkled my nose and closed it again. "What's that stink?"

"There are sour-gas wells around here somewhere," Uncle Jamie said. "Sometimes they smell like that." He peered out the window at the smoke, which had already started to drift away. "That smoke is dying off. Some rancher is probably burning deadfall or something."

"In the rain?" I asked.

"Well, it would keep the risk of a grass fire down, keep it easier to contain. Probably smart to do it in the rain," Uncle Jamie said.

"Hmm." My mind had already gone back to the race and what had happened to Kelsey. The whole thing was crazy. She was such a good rider—crashing like that seemed weird. I mean, I knew anyone could crash. But still...

The gravel road turned into the highway, and the miles rolled by. Eventually the adrenaline ebbed away, and I fell asleep with my face against the window.

"Mitch?" I felt a gentle shake on my shoulder. I blinked.

"Huh?" I sat up and drew in a breath. "Are we there?"

"Yes. Come on. I texted Kelsey's mom. They have her in Emergency right now."

The hospital doors slid shut behind us, and I looked for any sign of Kelsey. Uncle Jamie had started toward the nurses' station when Kelsey's mom stepped out of a side door.

"Jamie!" she called quietly, and we both turned.

"How is she?" I blurted. "Is Kelsey okay?"

Her mom's lips pressed into a thin line. She swallowed. "They don't think her ribs are broken," she said, but before I could draw a breath of relief, she went on. "They think she has damaged her kidneys and lacerated her liver. They're getting ready to airlift her to Calgary right now."

Uncle Jamie gave Kelsey's mom a quick hug. "I'm sure she's going to be fine."

Kelsey's mom nodded silently. She swallowed hard again before she spoke. "They'll be loading her into the ambulance and taking her to the airport."

This sounded really bad to me. Way worse than broken ribs. "Where is she? Can we see her?"

"I don't think there's time. They're getting her ready to go. But come with me and we'll see." We followed Kelsey's mom back through the Emergency section. Kelsey was already on a gurney and being wheeled out. We followed as the paramedics hurried her through a large exit door where an ambulance was waiting.

They hoisted her into the ambulance so quickly, I couldn't even get close enough to say goodbye. But Kelsey turned her head at the last second and caught my eye. In spite of the tubes and medical stuff all over the place, she managed a grin and gave me a thumbs-up.

And I knew what that meant. She was no quitter, and she would be okay.

Chapter Fourteen

"Mitch?" My mom poked her head around my bedroom door. "Dad's on the phone. He wants to say hi to you." She couldn't hide the worry on her face.

This was the one thing I'd been dreading for the past three days. I rolled off the bed, where I'd been staring at the ceiling. I took the phone from her.

"Thanks," I said.

I'd had a difficult time explaining why my dirt bike wasn't in the truck when we finally made it home after the race and

Kelsey's accident. Both my mom and Uncle Jamie were upset, but they knew how tough the whole race had been, so they left it alone. I heard Uncle Jamie tell my mom to give me a few days and then we'd talk about it some more. I didn't know what there was to talk about. I'd lost the race and lost my bike. Period. End of story.

"Hi, Dad," I said. "How's it going?"

"Not bad. I've had a busy few days."

"Oh yeah? Doing what?" I didn't really mean to sound sarcastic, but even to me I did. Kind of like I was accusing him of not being here when I needed him. Or maybe I did mean to. I don't even know.

There was a pause. "Well, the whole pipeline project is getting delayed because of environmental issues. I have activists coming out of my ears up here, and I completely get why they're concerned. I've got a whole team doing absolutely everything they can to make sure the pipeline is safe and won't leak. But some of the people who don't agree with it just won't listen to anything we say. A few of them are even trying to sabotage the project."

"What do you mean?" I said. I wasn't really listening. I rolled onto my bed again and went back to staring at the ceiling.

"Well, like vandalizing equipment. We've just had some problems, that's all." Dad paused again. "Mom told me you've had a few problems yourself."

"Yeah."

"Want to talk about it?" he asked.

"Not really."

"You might feel better."

"I doubt it."

"I wish I was there," Dad said.

I didn't say anything.

"Mitch?"

"I wish you were here too," I said, my voice thick with tears I refused to let show.

"I heard you lost the dirt bike in a bet."

"Yeah. This guy Logan kind of pushed me into it. He said a bunch of stuff, but mostly he said that how we bought the bike in the first place wasn't exactly legal.

He said Uncle Jamie could get in trouble for it. I didn't want that to happen."

"Why wouldn't it be legal?"

"He crashed hard that day. He said maybe he had a concussion and wasn't thinking clearly. That maybe Uncle Jamie took advantage of him."

"Hmm. I doubt that's true. But okay. So you were worried and agreed to the new terms?"

"Yeah. Whoever placed higher in their class got the bike. And I stopped racing to help Kelsey get out of the bush and find help. So I lost."

"I know. I heard the whole story."

I waited, sure that the fact I had wasted two thousand dollars and tons of Uncle Jamie's and Darren's time fixing it was the next part of the lecture.

"You know, Mitch..." Dad started. I braced myself for his next words. "I've never been more proud of you."

"What?" I said, startled out of my bummed-out state.

"It takes a lot of courage to face the risks Kelsey had to deal with out there, and you stayed and saw her through it. And knowing what it meant to you to lose the race, you were incredibly unselfish as well."

"But she's my friend. Of course I would stay and help her."

"Some wouldn't. They would have let the sweepers bring her in so they could keep racing."

"I never even thought of that."

"Exactly. Which is why I'm so proud. You showed a lot of character doing that. Plus, you were probably scared. You've never had to deal with a medical emergency before, and you did the very best you could. From what your mom said, Kelsey could easily have died out there."

"Yeah," I whispered. I didn't ever want to think about that again.

"So it cost a bunch of money, which sucks, and this Logan guy sounds like a real jerk, but it is what it is. You stood up and helped a friend when it really counted, and that's more important than any amount of money."

"You really mean that?" I asked.

"I really do," Dad said.

I swallowed. "Thanks."

"I love you, Mitch."

"Love you too, Dad."

I showered and found some clean jeans. Uncle Jamie was coming to pick me up. Kelsey was finally allowed visitors outside of family today.

The doorbell rang. Usually Uncle Jamie rings the bell three or four times and then walks in—kind of just to let us know he's barging in on us. But this time I didn't hear him come in. I ran down the stairs and yanked open the door. "Hey, you could have just come in, you know—" I started, then stopped.

It was Logan standing there on the porch. "Hi," he said.

"Hi."

"I heard about Kelsey." Logan shifted from foot to foot.

"Yeah?" I wasn't sure where this was going.

"Yeah. And I found your dirt bike at my campsite. We had to pack and go, and I heard about the accident but I didn't know that's why you DNF'd, so I just left."

"DNF'd?"

"Did Not Finish. Man, you really haven't raced, have you?"

"No. I told you that."

"Anyway. I thought about it, and I don't think the bet was fair. You stopped to help her and sacrificed your own race. I think we should redo it."

"What?"

"I think we should redo the race. The second Porcupine Hills race is in two weeks. It's a hare scramble instead of a cross-country, so that'll be better for you, because the loop is much shorter. I'll even ride the course with you the day before, if you want."

"Why would you do that?" I shook my head.

"Because it took real guts to do what you did, getting Kelsey out of there. And anyone who does something like that deserves a second chance at getting his bike back. Do we have a deal?" Logan stuck out his hand.

"I guess so," I said, completely blown away by this turn of events.

"Good. Help me unload it. You'll need to start practicing." Logan stepped to the side so I could see the driveway and my dirt bike strapped down in the back of his truck.

Chapter Fifteen

Darren led Uncle Jamie and me through the crowded lobby to the long row of hospital elevators. People were everywhere. People who carried flowers, people who looked worried, people wearing pale scrubs who were doctors or nurses.

I clutched the bag I had for Kelsey a little tighter. I didn't want to bring flowers. Darren had bought a big bouquet of yellow sunflowers on the way up to the hospital. Instead, I got her a little toy dirt bike, an orange one like her own. I thought she'd like that to look at more than a stuffed animal or more flowers.

The elevator dinged, and everyone surged inside. When we hit our floor, I had to fight my way out.

"She's over this way," Darren said. We walked down a hallway, past a nurses' station, around a bunch of equipment and chairs and to Kelsey's room.

"Hey!" Kelsey smiled as soon as we walked in. She was wearing a hoodie and sitting up in bed, a dirt-biking magazine spread out on the blankets. She still looked pale.

"Hey, you." Darren put the sunflowers on her lap. "How's it going?"

"I'm so bored," Kelsey answered. "Thanks, they're beautiful," she added, smelling the flowers. "Did you bring something to put them in?"

"Jeez, no, I forgot," said Darren.

"That's okay. Just fill that metal thing up with water and stick them in there for now." Kelsey gestured to a shallow metal bowl with what looked like a built-in toilet seat on top.

"You want me to use the bedpan?" Darren started to laugh.

"It's not like I'm going to use it," Kelsey said. "The doctors want me to stay still, but I'm getting up to go to the bathroom, no matter what. I'm *never* peeing in that thing."

"Okay." Darren shrugged, took the bedpan over to the sink, filled it with water and stuffed the sunflowers in.

"Looks great," Kelsey said.

I handed her the little dirt bike. "I brought you something too," I said.

"Oooh, that's cool," she said. "I can do jumps off my knee." She ran the dirt bike over her leg and made it sail through the air. "I haven't played with mini bikes since I was, like, ten. But thanks. There's not much to do here."

"Where are your mom and dad?" Uncle Jamie asked.

"Mom's out getting food. Dad went back to the farm. He left this morning, but he'll probably come in again tomorrow."

"Did they say how long you'll be here?" Darren asked.

Kelsey made a face. "A while. They said I lacerated my liver, which means I cut it up pretty bad. And one kidney isn't looking good. It might come back, or it might die off. We don't know yet."

"What happens if it dies?" I said, horrified.

"Not much," Kelsey said. "A person can live just fine with one kidney."

An awkward silence fell. We all knew she was trying to be brave, but we also knew this likely meant racing was over for her.

"Kel, you need anything?" Darren said. "We can go get you some snacks or whatever."

"Oh, that would be great! Would you mind? The food here is awful. Mom is picking up dinner, but I could really use some juice for at night, and maybe some granola bars or something."

"Sure. Jamie and I can go down to the coffee shop and see what there is," Darren said.

When they had left, I turned to her. "Okay, truth. How are you really?"

"This completely sucks, and it hurts," she said. "But I'm okay. It'll be a while before I can ride again though."

"If ever," I said.

"What's that supposed to mean?" she demanded.

"Well, if everything heals, isn't it still too risky to get on a dirt bike? What if you crashed again?"

"What if I didn't?" she countered.

"Everyone crashes. You were the one who told me that."

"True, but I can wear a kidney belt. There's equipment to protect you."

"Still too risky."

"What are you, my mother?"

"No, your friend. And I don't want to see you get hurt."

"Too late."

"Exactly." We glared at each other. I took a breath. "Look, let's just see what the doctors say. There's no point fighting about it."

Kelsey sank back onto the pillow. "I know. I'm just scared. Racing has been a huge part of my life. What if I really can't?"

"Then you'll do something else. Trust me, you're not the type to sit around for long."

We sat in silence. There didn't seem to be much more to say.

"I don't want to quit," Kelsey said at last.

"I know," I said.

Kelsey blew out a huge breath. "Ow!" she said. "That hurt."

Uncle Jamie stepped back into the room, his arms full of drinks. "I didn't know what you like, so I got you one of everything," he said.

Kelsey laughed. "Looks like you bought the whole store."

"Almost." Uncle Jamie grinned. "Wait until Darren gets here. He got even more stuff than I did."

"You guys didn't have to do that," Kelsey said. "Honestly."

"We wanted to. Hey, Mitch, turn the television up. The news is on. I want to hear the weather."

"You could check your phone." I reached for the remote and turned up the volume.

Uncle Jamie didn't bother to answer, because Darren arrived then with a grocery bag full of fruit and muffins and all kinds of things. I listened to the news to see if they were going to report the weather, but the only thing they were talking about was a fire that had destroyed a truck at some sour-gas well south of Calgary.

"RCMP are still investigating, but they have confirmed that arson was the cause of the fire. There are currently no suspects in the case. Anyone with information is asked to call RCMP immediately," said the newscaster.

I clicked the television off. "There's nothing on," I told Uncle Jamie, who was rearranging the drinks and snacks for Kelsey along the shelf by her bed. He was fussing so much, he reminded me of a little old lady.

"Come on, Grandma," I told him. "Since when do you care about everything being neat and tidy?"

"I'm very particular about these kinds of things." Uncle Jamie grinned. "Now Kelsey can reach whatever she needs without getting up. It's all organized." He gave her a gentle hug. "We better let you rest."

"Yeah," Darren added, hugging her as well. "We'll come and see you again soon. Take care of yourself."

"Thanks for coming, guys," Kelsey said. As Darren and Uncle Jamie headed for the door, I turned back.

"And I'll see *you* on the racetrack," Kelsey whispered.

I couldn't help but smile.

Chapter Sixteen

The morning sparkled with early sunlight. Birds chirped, and a fresh wind breezed through the pine trees.

I wanted to puke.

Why had I ever wanted to race dirt bikes? I was more nervous now than at the last race. I glanced at my bike on the stand beside the trailer. I sure was glad to have it back, but it would hurt even more if I lost it twice. And the memory of Kelsey curled up on the cold ground in the trees was hard to erase. I knew I had to get that

Kick Start

image out of my head if I wanted to race today. I'd never make it through if I kept thinking about the accident.

"Hey." Logan stepped around the side of the trailer.

"Hi," I said, startled. He was the last person I expected to see.

"You want to go for a ride?" he asked.

"Now?"

"Sure. Riders' meeting isn't until ten o'clock. It's only seven thirty. We could go for an hour or so."

I was having a hard time believing this was the same guy I had bought the bike from.

He grinned and held up his hands. "Trust me, I'm not going to sabotage you or anything. I just thought you might want to do a practice ride. I said that, remember, when I brought your bike back."

"I didn't think you were serious."

"Well, I was," Logan said. "So do you want to go?"

"Okay. I have to get my gear."

"Meet me at my trailer when you're ready." Logan turned and walked away.

I pulled my gear bag out of the back of the truck. Everything in it felt freezing cold from being outside all night. I kept my socks and boots in the tent trailer, but there was no room for the rest of it in there. I stripped down and pulled on the knee guards, elbow guards, neck brace, jersey, pants, chest protector, socks and boots, helmet, goggles...I needed a checklist to remember everything. I could barely move when I had it all on.

I stuck my head inside the trailer. "I'm going for a quick ride," I told Uncle Jamie. "I'll be back before riders' meeting."

"Okay," Uncle Jamie said blearily, reaching for the instant coffee.

I started my bike and putted over the grass toward Logan's trailer.

He was waiting for me. He shifted his bike into gear and rode ahead, leading me toward the trees where the kids' races had started last time. "Let's head up this trail. It should cross over the race course at the top." He buzzed straight up through the trees, zigzagging his back tire over the roots.

I shook my head, clearing my thoughts. It would be a challenge, but this time I wasn't backing down from anything. I cranked the throttle and followed him, doing my best to keep up. We crested the hill, and I was amazed that I had done it. It had actually seemed easy.

Logan stopped at the top and waited for me. "The trail is flagged over there for the kids' races. We'll just go around it so you can practice. We're not really supposed to ride the actual course."

"It wouldn't be fair to the other riders if I knew the course in advance," I said.

"No. Lots of people do it, but we'll stick to the rules. Come on!" Logan gunned the engine and took off. I followed him, weaving through the trees.

Logan was very, very good. I watched what he did ahead of me and tried to mimic it. We sailed over dips and spun around turns, and the miles flew by. When he pulled to a stop, I had only one thought.

Had he taken me out to teach me to be a better rider or to exhaust me before the race? Because I was wiped out, and we still had a ways to go yet. Maybe I had fallen for a trick after all.

"Getting tired?" Logan asked.

"Yeah, a bit," I said.

"Excellent. We'll cut back just ahead here. You can grab something to eat, and by the time you race, you'll be warmed up and good to go."

I sucked on the mouthpiece of my backpack water carrier. "Hope so," I said.

"Trust me," Logan said. He wheeled his bike around. "It's a bit steep going down over here, but it's the fastest way back to camp. Just take it slow, and you'll be all right." He edged his bike through the bush on the ridge and then dropped down.

This place looked familiar. I thought we were near where Kelsey had crashed, but it was hard to tell. Trees and bushes can look a lot alike. I edged down the steep incline after Logan. My back tire skidded, and suddenly the bike was going down. I panicked

and released the clutch, which made it stall.
I got my footing and hauled the bike back
up, put it in neutral and started it again.

"You okay?" Logan yelled up to me.

"Yeah!" I answered. I crept forward
again, more cautiously. The bike rolled
slowly forward, and I kept my feet out,
touching the ground as I made my way
down. I breathed a sigh of relief as I pulled
up beside Logan.

"Should be easier now. We'll follow this
trail. It levels out after a while. We'll hit the
gravel road and head back," Logan said.

"Okay." I took another gulp of water
and paused to look around. This area
did look familiar. And way off to the left,
where the hill dipped even steeper, I saw a
pink ribbon flapping in the breeze, tied to
a bush. "Logan," I said.

"Yeah?"

"Is that race marker supposed to be
there?" I had a weird feeling in my stomach.
I pointed to the ribbon.

Logan looked. He frowned. "I don't
think so," he said. He leaned his bike

against a tree. "Let's check it out." He walked toward the ribbon.

I propped up my bike too and followed him. The terrain was difficult even for walking—slick and steep and full of roots. I had to grab a bush to keep from sliding. When we reached the ribbon, we were able to see down the hill. It was so steep, it was almost a cliff, strewn with gray shale. Another pink ribbon fluttered midway down, tied to a tiny shrub. I turned and glanced up. A few yards away, near the top of the steep incline, a third ribbon danced in the breeze.

Logan and I stared at each other. "This is definitely a problem," he said.

Chapter Seventeen

"Something's not right," Logan said.
"There's no way a hill like this would be
flagged for a race course. Especially for the
kids' classes."

"What do you think is going on?" I
asked.

"I don't know. But I think we better look
around and see if this really is the race flag-
ging," Logan said. "Sorry, dude. I know this
is a harder trail back than we planned."

We trekked back and started the bikes.
I rode toward the first pink ribbon we

had seen. I was really not sure I could do this. The shale slipped dangerously under the tires. I felt like I had no control.

"Go down!" Logan yelled, gesturing down the cliff. "I'm going up top to have a look."

Go down. Yeah, right. My palms started sweating just looking at the steep monster ahead of me. I started but slid on the shale, and I cut to the side. Maybe I could try carving back and forth, like I was skiing, instead of going straight down.

That worked better. Inch by inch I worked sideways, zigzagging until I lost my balance and dumped the bike, landing sideways on my butt. Cursing under my breath, I picked up the bike and didn't even bother trying to start it again. I kept my hand on the brake and walked it down, rolling it a little at a time, until I reached the pink ribbon at the bottom. Once I was down I stopped for a breather, flipping my goggles up. To my dismay, another pink ribbon waved from a branch a few yards away.

I heard the rumble of an engine above me, and Logan appeared at the crest of the hill. Without hesitating, he drove the bike over the edge, sliding down through the shale and dirt, raising a cloud of dust behind him. He cut sideways here and there but stuck mostly to the trail, ending up beside in me in about two seconds—a trip that had taken me at least fifteen minutes.

"Hey," he said, stopping.

"Hey," I said. Man, I sucked at this.

"There are more flags up there," he said.

"There's another down here." I pointed to the one a few yards away.

"I don't get it. This is way too advanced for a kids' course," said Logan. "Even for the men's races, this is pretty dangerous. The pros could do it, and the intermediates, but that's about it."

"Do you think it's a mistake?" I said.

"It has to be," said Logan.

"Unless this is an old course from a different race?" I suggested.

Logan shook his head and got off his bike. "Have a look at this," he said, pulling the branch that held the pink ribbon nearest us. "If this ribbon had been here a while, it would be dirty and faded. It looks brand-new."

"Except that it's a bit ripped and crunched up," I said, leaning in for a closer look. Logan released the branch, and it snapped back.

"Let's go a bit farther and see if we can spot more ribbons," I said.

"I hope not. The creek should be just ahead. If they've put them there, that's even worse," Logan said.

We rode down through the trees and found two more ribbons guiding us toward the creek. Sure enough, another ribbon fluttered on the other side.

"That water is too high to cross here. This is totally wrong," Logan said.

I squinted, searching the other side to see if more pink ribbons were visible, but the trees obscured anything else.

"We have to ride back and let the race organizers know," Logan said. "The only thing I can think of is that they've switched the courses around to have the kids start on the other side, where the men raced last time. But it doesn't make much sense...the trails over there are harder and much longer. The kids' track has always been on this side of the creek, but never down this way. The loop is different each time, but they keep the kids on the flatter ground, along the back of the private land."

Private land.

Those two words rang in my brain, and suddenly so many thoughts collided, I couldn't focus on just one.

The signs on the fence that warned people away.

The woman who came out of the ranch house, yelling at Kelsey and me to get our filthy machines off her property.

The pink ribbon that looked brand-new but was ripped and crumpled, like it had been untied and retied again.

The race trail flagged through deadly terrain *that had never been flagged this way before.*

"Logan, how far away from private land are we?" I asked.

"Uh, not far, I don't think."

"Can you get us to where the kids' loop would usually run near there?" I said.

"Yeah, but why?" Logan asked.

"I'll explain when we get there, if I'm right," I said.

"Okay, but we have to hurry. Riders' meeting is in, like, an hour," said Logan. He turned the bike away from the creek and rode west. Thankfully, he didn't take the trail back up the cliff. I followed him, pushing myself to keep up. Within minutes we emerged from the trees, scooted up a slope and found the barbed-wire fence decorated with threatening signs.

"Where's the kids' loop?" I asked.

"This way!" Logan skirted the fence, backtracking. When we hit the ridge, he headed east. We soon rode into a treed area and followed a trail that now was familiar. It only took a few minutes to find what we were looking for—a stray pink ribbon, new, bright and untouched.

"The kids' loop *is* over here," Logan said, stopping his bike. "I don't get it."

"I do," I said grimly.

"What?" Logan looked at me.

"Someone moved the course. On purpose. Someone who doesn't like dirt bikers and doesn't want us racing anywhere near her land—and would prefer we weren't racing at all."

"What are you talking about?" Logan asked.

I told him everything I suspected. How the rancher had ranted at us and refused to help when Kelsey was hurt, how I had seen threatening protest signs in the shed when we'd stopped to rest, all the signs along the fence.

"I think she's an environmental activist, and I think she's fed up with us racing out here. She's decided to do something to put a stop to it," I said. "I can't prove it, but how else do you explain the kids' loop suddenly turning away from her ranch and tracking down into such sketchy terrain? And what's really scary is, someone could get badly hurt. Look at what happened to Kelsey." I wondered briefly if what had happened to her was from reflagging in that race too, but I quickly put that thought away. I had no way to check it out, let alone prove it now.

"We have to get back," Logan said. "Now. Before the race starts."

"You better go. You're way faster than me, You'll get there in half the time," I said, my heart thumping at the idea of navigating my way back alone.

"You sure?" Logan said.

"Yeah. Go," I said.

"Okay. See you back there." Logan kicked at the starter, hard.

Nothing happened.

Chapter Eighteen

Logan swore and jumped on the kick-starter again. Still nothing. "What's the matter with this thing?" He climbed off the bike.

"There's gas in the tank," I said.

Logan shook his head. "It could be a spark plug that's dead. Or dirt in the fuel line. Never mind. I've got tools—I'll fix it. You go."

"Me?"

"Someone has to stop the race before it starts. It has to be you," Logan said.

"You could take my bike," I suggested. "You're faster than I am."

"That would leave you stranded out here with mine. And I'm guessing you don't know how to fix it."

"No," I admitted. "But how do you know that you do?"

"I don't. But it's not the first time I've had a bike crap out on me in the bush. I have an extra spark plug in my toolkit. I'll check everything, and if I'm lucky I'll get it going and catch up to you."

"And if you're not lucky?"

"You'll send someone back to find me. Head straight west until you hit the gravel road, then go north until you get to the camp. You know you're going west if you can see the mountains straight ahead of you."

"That's a lot of help if I'm stuck in the trees!" I said.

"You'll figure it out. Just go!" Logan urged.

I started my bike and spun the back wheel around so I could go back the way we had come. I cranked the throttle, and the bike jerked forward. I held on and shot into the trees, weaving crazily on the trail. My heart thumped, and my palms sweated so much my gloves felt wet. I wasn't even sure I could find my way back to camp, let alone get there in time to stop the race. I stood up on the pegs for more stability and focused everything I had on the trail and the bike, willing myself to tackle it faster. I backtracked to the fence with the signs. As I hurtled along the path, I saw the break in the fence where Kelsey and I had gone through. For just a heartbeat, I considered cutting through the land. It was tempting... I knew the ranch house was near the gravel road.

But there was also a chance I'd run into the rancher. I didn't want to do that again.

I decided to keep going along the fence line, at least for a while. I figured it must eventually end or turn or something, and I'd end up near the road. The path hugged the fence, so it wasn't really difficult to ride. It just seemed to go on forever.

I rode. And I rode. And I rode. I was beginning to regret not cutting through the break in the fence when finally it turned, and then there was no fence, just trees. I wondered what the heck had happened... was I still on public land? I slowed down to get my bearings, and suddenly a woman stepped onto the trail right in front of me. I braked hard, my back wheel skidding out.

"Hey!" I cried. "Be careful!"

"*You* be careful!" the woman snapped back. I recognized her right away. She was the rancher who had yelled at me and Kelsey when we crossed her land.

She was carrying a red gasoline can that looked heavy. "You have no business being here," she said.

"I'm on public property," I replied. "And I'm in a hurry. There's danger...kids who—"

"You're on *my* land," the woman interrupted. "And I want you and your dirty, polluting, destructive machine off it...*now*!"

"Gladly!" I said, suddenly so angry that I hit the throttle and mud flew off my back tire in a shower of dirt. I left her standing there holding her gasoline can and sputtering as I sped off, my hands shaking with rage.

I raced through the trees and within seconds emerged into a clearing. There were trucks and equipment and a few structures and buildings. I didn't know where I was, but I knew one thing: where there were trucks, there would be a road. Or a driveway, at least, that led to a road. I circled around the facility, found the driveway and rode hard. I was relieved that I'd finally found my way out.

Then I saw the locked gate a few yards away from the gravel road and the barbed-wire fence on either side of it.

I wanted to yell or hit something. I was so close! I could see the gravel road on the other side. But how was I supposed to get there? I didn't want to backtrack through that woman's property or, worse, back to where I had left Logan. I'd never make it to the camp in time to stop the race!

There had to be a way through. I wondered if I could drag the dirt bike underneath the gate. It was just a simple bar system meant to stop cars. The bottom bar was pretty low, but I thought I could do it.

I tipped the bike sideways, and it immediately began leaking fuel. I quickly shut the valve and tried again, but the handlebars were just too wide. This wasn't going to work.

I wondered if I should leave the bike and go on foot, but I'd never make it in time that way either.

Okay then. If I couldn't go under, maybe I could go over. The gate wasn't that high. If I could find something to use as a ramp, I could make a jump.

Jeez, who was I kidding? I was such a chicken. Kelsey could take a jump like that no problem, and so could Logan. But not me. I chewed on my lip, trying to push away the thought of Kelsey curled up on the ground in pain. If I didn't do something soon, the kids who were about to race could be in the same situation. Maybe worse.

But there was nothing to make a ramp with anyway. Just a bunch of rocks and logs in the ditch.

I looked down the road in the direction I needed to go, but the barbed wire stretched as far as I could see. So I couldn't go under it, couldn't go over it, couldn't go around it. I'd have to go through it. Wasn't there a song about this?

Except I couldn't go through it either. I didn't have any wire cutters or anything with me.

But I had to do something. I glanced at the debris in the ditch and thought of the first time I had seen Kelsey ride. I'd watched her make her way through a whole section of rocks and logs that stretched up like a ramp to the trail. Could I somehow do the same?

I looked again at the gate. One end was sagging. I started hauling the biggest rocks I could lift out of the ditch and piling them at the sagging end. I dumped smaller logs on top sideways and tried to wedge them in to make a secure bridge. I had to pile them on both sides of the gate, because there was no way I'd have enough speed to take it as a jump. I'd have to be steady and handle it as an obstacle. It didn't take long, because the gate was only a few feet high at that end. I made sure the rocks on each side held the pile in place so nothing would move.

This was a really bad idea. I knew it was. But I also knew I had no choice. I could hear Kelsey's voice in my head. *Just go for it*, she was saying. *Hit the throttle and do it.*

I had to stop thinking and go. I backed up, eyed my contraption and rode toward the ramp. The front wheel hit the first log and the bike pitched sideways. I touched my feet down and gave it more gas, willing the bike to straighten and get the momentum to go up and over. If I got stuck, I'd never get over it. I had to power through it.

The bike lurched. Even though the gate wasn't very high, I felt so far from the ground that I didn't dare look at the ground. My heart in my throat, I pushed hard with my feet and gassed the bike harder. I felt the logs slip. I held my breath. The bike shot forward and over the gate just as my ramp began to fall apart. The logs on the downward slope held, and the bike floated over it and came to rest on the flat dirt.

My whole body was shaking, and I was breathing hard, sucking in air. *I did it.* I could barely take time to celebrate, though, because now there was no time to waste.

Chapter Nineteen

The gravel road should have been an easy ride. And it was, except that I'd only gone a short distance before I caught a whiff of smoke. I glanced back and saw black puffs rising into the sky, right where I had ridden out of the woods.

I turned my attention to the road. Gravel is a slippery, dangerous thing to ride a motorcycle on, and I wasn't about to wipe out after everything I'd been through. But as I rode, the smoke triggered other memories. Smoke on another occasion, the day Kelsey had crashed...and the smell of rotten eggs. The television news in the hospital about an unsolved arson fire at a sour-gas well south of Calgary.

And a woman who'd railed against polluters carrying a gasoline can toward the buildings and equipment I had just left. I didn't know if that place had a sour-gas well, but I was pretty sure I was right about that woman being involved. And if I was, I had two crimes to stop.

I gunned the engine and concentrated on staying on two wheels. The campsites couldn't be that much farther ahead.

The first colors of the trailers flashed through the trees. I veered off the road toward the race organizers' trailers. No one was there. The riders' meeting must have ended. The campsites were empty.

Which meant everyone was at the starts, getting ready to race. I couldn't take all this stress! I wheeled around and hit the throttle, ignoring the speed postings for the campground. I buzzed up the dirt path, across the gravel road and toward the kids' starting point. The Expert Kids were already lined up. One of the organizers grabbed the flag. I pinned the throttle hard, weaving up the trail, and braked hard in front of the line, sending a shower of dust spraying into the air.

"Stop!" I yelled, ripping my goggles off my face. "You have to stop the race!"

Chapter Twenty

My nerves were shot. I had ridden terrain I'd never thought I could, left my riding partner in the woods with a broken-down bike and navigated alone. I had built my own endurocross logs section, caught a criminal red-handed and ridden back to camp in fourth gear, wide open.

And I hadn't even raced yet.

Logan sipped a can of orange juice. "You are one ballsy kid," he said.

"I was scared out of my mind," I said.

"Everybody is," Logan replied. "No matter how good a rider you are, you're always scared if you challenge yourself. You just push the fear away and do it anyway."

I thought about this. I had always believed that when you were really skilled, you weren't scared anymore. But maybe fear is part of the game.

"The sweepers are back. They reflagged the course," Logan said. "The races should be starting soon."

"Is your bike okay to race?" I asked.

"Yeah, it should be fine. There was just dirt in the fuel line. I don't think it will be a problem now."

Logan had pulled into the campground a few minutes after I had stopped the race. He had managed to clear the fuel line and get the bike going, and then he'd back-tracked the way we had come instead of pushing forward like I had.

Logan cleared his throat. "You know, you really deserve that bike. You've earned it. If you don't want to race after everything that happened this morning, that's okay."

I stood up. "No. We had a deal. I'm racing. And I'm keeping that bike fair and square." We both grinned.

The horn sounded, indicating it was time to go to our starting positions.

I stuck out my hand. Logan shook it. "Good luck," I said.

"You too," he answered.

I pulled on my helmet and started my bike. Confidence flooded me. There wasn't anything on this race that could possibly be harder than what I had already done today.

"See you after," I said and revved my bike. I shifted into gear and sped up to the starting point. The usual muddle of riders didn't phase me. I pulled into position and waited for my class's turn at the line. The afternoon sun warmed my face. The races were late starting because of the reflagging. After I had told the organizers everything that had happened, someone immediately drove out to get cell service and called the RCMP. They reported the fire and the deliberate changes to the race course. The sweepers had to chart a whole new course for the kids' race, because the original had to stay intact until the RCMP could investigate. So I had no idea where we were going, but I didn't care. The fun and excitement of racing out in the woods filled me. There were new friends here to meet, and Uncle Jamie cheering me on. I wished Kelsey and my dad could be here.

But there was always next time.

I pulled up to the checkpoint. One of the volunteers scanned my helmet. "You're done!" she shouted into my ear, over the rumble of bike engines.

I pulled off to the side, where Uncle Jamie waited, and stripped off my filthy goggles.

"How was it?" Uncle Jamie asked as I cut the motor.

"Hard," I said, mud cracking at the corners of my mouth. My pants were coated with mud and soaked from the thighs down. I'd bogged down in a puddle and fallen into the sludge. Other riders had spattered up dirt and mud when they passed me, plastering my jersey with it. On the dry stretches, dust had smothered the air. I could feel it in my nostrils and coating my face. My gloves were wet, my palms blistered. My knee hurt where I had hit it on a tree when I tried to pass someone. My butt was chafed raw from the bike seat.

I felt great!

"It was hard, but awesome!" I told him. "Where did I place?"

"I think fourth, but it's not official until they post it," Uncle Jamie said.

"Fourth!" I said, stunned. Out of thirteen kids, placing fourth for my second race ever was incredible! "Wow," I said.

"Yeah!" Uncle Jamie clapped me on the shoulder. "Pretty amazing, Mitch. I'm so stoked for you!"

"Me too!" I glanced around. "Did Logan come in yet?"

"The Intermediate Men's finish is on the other side, so I don't know. Probably not. They have a longer loop, and they race for two and a half hours. He'll probably be a while."

"Okay." I started the bike and pulled away from the gas-up area. "I'm heading over there to wait."

"Sure. I'll meet you at the trailer then." Uncle Jamie picked up our gas can and the bag of extra gear.

I bumped slowly down the trail through the trees, heading toward the campsite. My whole body ached. A sandwich and a shower sounded like heaven right now.

But that would have to wait. I rolled into the checkpoint for the men's and ladies' classes. A few riders were in, but I guessed they had stopped early, judging from the repairs being made to the bikes and the people buzzing around them. Spectators milled about, talking and waiting for riders. Since it was near the end of the race, no one was standing by the fuel cans for the riders to come in and gas up. The sun shone hot now, and flies buzzed in the trees. As soon as I got off the bike and sat down on a log, they swarmed around me, attracted by the salty sweat on my face.

I shooed them away and waited. The distant hum of bikes became louder. I watched as some of the riders emerged from the trees. They all wore as much mud as I did, and they looked as tired as I felt. Logan was not among them.

I felt a twinge of uneasiness. Logan was fast. He should be coming in with the top riders. I couldn't tell which riders were in his class, but as more and more made it through the final check, I began to wonder. I was just about to go and ask at the checkpoint if anyone had seen him on the trail when the familiar colors of his gear zipped among the branches on the trail.

He raced under the awning of the last checkpoint. They scanned him, and he pulled out, looking for an open place to stop the bike. I waved at him. He rode toward me, killed the engine and yanked off his helmet.

"That was a ride!" he said. "I ate it twice on the trail, once in the mud."

"Me too," I said. "Your bike okay?"

"I stalled it in the mud and got dirt in the fuel line *again*," Logan said. "That, like, should never happen."

I waited. Logan stared at me. He knew, and I knew, what was on my mind.

"So they told me I placed eighth when I came in," Logan said. "Unofficially."

A bubble of happiness swelled in my chest. "Unofficially, I placed fourth."

Logan grinned and stuck out his hand. "Congratulations." We shook hands, a muddy, wet handshake that meant more than anything.

I looked at my dirt bike, propped up on a log. Filthy, still unfinished, it was the most wonderful sight in the world.

Because it was *mine*.

At last.

Acknowledgments

Kick Start, in particular the character of Kelsey Murray, is based on a true story.

When she was sixteen, Shelby Turner crashed her bike during a race. The courage and sheer grit it took for her to get herself off the mountain despite being severely injured were the inspiration for this story.

A big thank-you is due to Renee Turner, Shelby's mother, for supplying the details of what happened that day in the woods, and to Bernice Wilton, who worked with me on the elements of the race. None of us who were at that race will ever forget it.

Heartfelt thanks go out as well to Mike, Matthew and Jordan Bossley for their patient instruction on the inner workings of dirt bikes and their detailed recollections of racing; Ethan Bossley for his input on what teenage boys would read and what is actually cool; and Andrew Bossley for helping me edit the manuscript.

Thanks are also due to Tanya Trafford, for her excellent input on the manuscript, and all the Orca team who worked so hard on this book.

And lastly, the biggest thank-you of all goes to Shelby Turner for letting me use her story. Her determination and continued success are truly inspiring. Today she is one of the top female riders in North America and has competed in the most challenging motocross, off-road and endurocross events the racing world has to offer, including the X Games and the International Six Days of Enduro.

Michele Martin Bossley is the author of numerous books for young people, including *Jumper* and *Kicker* in the Orca Sports series. When not writing, she can be found watching her four sons competing in dirt-bike racing and many other sports. She lives in Calgary.